Keith Ryzor had intended to meet Madeline for their third date, but at the last second, she cancels. Already at the restaurant, he decides to head in and eat at the bar. He spots a man alone with a beer and a plate of hot wings. Noticing the bit of hot sauce reddening the black man's closely-cropped goatee, Keith sits down next to him and tells him about it. While he knows it's not the most standard way to strike up a conversation, the guy doesn't seem to mind. Keith finds himself sharing a surprisingly enjoyable meal with a man named Oliver Kostroma. Even though Keith normally dates women, he's been with men, too, so he decides to ask him out. To his disappointment, Oliver turns him down.

Over the next week, Keith can't get the sexy electrician out of his mind. When Keith spots Oliver again in an unlikely place—at a barbeque of a co-worker's friend's house—he takes it as a sign. It's his second chance. Being a smart man, Keith learns from his mistakes. He doesn't ask Oliver out. Instead, he goes the friends route, which quickly adds in benefits. Knowing he's falling fast for Oliver, Keith enlists the aid of friends. Even as Keith works hard to win not only Oliver's trust, but his heart, there are also those working against him. Can Keith prove to the skittish man that he's worth the risk?

Cradling his Heart
Copyright © 2022 Charlie Richards
ISBN: 978-1-4874-1959-2
Cover art by Angela Waters

Published by eXtasy Books Inc

Look for us online at:
www.eXtasybooks.com

CRADLING HIS HEART
CARRY ME: BOOK TWELVE

BY

CHARLIE RICHARDS

DEDICATION

The beauty of love is that, you can fall in love with the most unex-
pected person at the most unexpected time.
~Rita Ghatourey

CHAPTER ONE

"I have a headache. I'm not going to make it. Sorry."

Tipping his head back, Keith rolled his eyes before frowning at the roof of his *BMW*. He sat in his vehicle, already at the restaurant. While he knew he was almost ten minutes early — he hated being late — his date could have called him an hour before to cancel, or even thirty minutes ago. Canceling ten minutes before a date was just damn rude. Plus, considering the woman lived in a high-rise in another part of town, she would have needed to leave home almost twenty minutes before to arrive on time.

This would have been Keith's third date with Madeline Lieman, and he'd thought they'd had a good connection.

And it doesn't help that she doesn't sound sorry.

Instead of sharing any of his thoughts, Keith forced a smile to his lips and kept his tone even. "I'm sorry to hear you're feeling poorly, Madeline. I hope you feel better soon."

"Thank you," Madeline replied, sounding a bit absent. "Perhaps we can try again Thursday evening?"

Narrowing his eyes, Keith evasively replied, "I'll need to check my schedule and call you back."

"Of course."

Before Madeline questioned him further, Keith continued, "I'll talk to you soon. Get some rest." Then he disconnected the call.

Keith made a mental note to have a late meeting on Thursday evening. Hating being stood up ranked right up there with being late. Regardless of Madeline's call, he still considered himself to be stood up.

His stomach growled.

"Well, I'm already here," Keith muttered, sliding his phone into the inside pocket of his suit jacket. "Let's get some chow."

Keith opened his door and stepped out of his *BMW*, closing the door after him. After buttoning his suit jacket, he locked his vehicle, tucked his keys into his pocket, and started toward the restaurant. Keith headed inside and stopped at the hostess stand.

"Good evening, sir," the young blond male greeted with a smile. "Do you have a reservation this evening?" He glanced beyond Keith and added, "Is it just you tonight, or are you waiting for the rest of your party?"

"I do have a reservation for this evening, for two, but I won't be needing it," Keith told the man. "It's under Keith Ryzor. Give another my table." Pointing toward the left, he added, "I'm just gonna sit at the bar."

The more Keith had spoken, the more the blond's eyes had widened. He glanced down at the stand, probably checking the reservation list. His cheeks even colored just a smidge, maybe because he'd noticed that when Keith had specified the reservation, he'd pre-ordered a bottle of their finest white to share with Madeline, having learned that it was her favorite.

"O-Of course, sir," the man stuttered. Then his brows furrowed as he asked, "Should I have the wine brought to the bar for you?"

With a shrug, Keith replied, "Why not."

Maybe he would call for an *Uber* after drinking it.

"Right away, sir," the host told him before turning away.

Keith grabbed a menu off the stand, then headed to the bar area. As he strolled inside, he took in the occupants. There was a dark-haired guy toward one end in a deep blue suit.

The cut didn't fit the guy quite right, and he saw the way the guy glanced around, as if he were casing the joint.

At the other end sat a black man in a pair of faded jeans, work boots, and a light-blue button-down. His long sleeves had been rolled up to above his elbows. He was focusing on the pile of hot wings before him while sparing the occasional glance at the TV mounted to the left of the bar.

Keith also couldn't help but notice the handsome man's lean features and the way his closely-cropped goatee framed his full lips. Full lips that opened so he could take a big bite of a chicken wing. When the handsome black man put down the wing bones and picked up his napkin, he rubbed over his lips.

The dab of hot sauce that Keith spotted when the guy lowered the napkin back to the bar drew a smile to Keith's lips. He started in the stranger's direction. He'd always been forward, and he found he couldn't help himself.

Settling on a stool, two to the right of the man, Keith placed the menu in front of him. He noticed the guy side-eye him ever-so-discreetly, but he didn't say anything to him. Keith did it for him.

Keith reached over the bar and grabbed a couple of cocktail napkins from the stack behind it. Holding one out to the man, he used the second one to point toward the dab of sauce still on the left side of his upper lip. Smiling just a smidge, Keith stated, "Missed a spot."

The guy slowly panned his attention to Keith. His focus flipped from him to the napkin and back again. Arching one thin black brow, he set down his chicken wing.

Then the man smirked and took the napkin. "Thanks," he murmured in a pleasantly mellow tenor. After he wiped over where Keith had indicated, surprisingly, he asked, "Did I get it?"

Keith grinned and nodded. "Yeah. You did." Holding out his hand, he offered, "I'm Keith. Keith Ryzor." When the man didn't immediately take his hand, Keith added, "My date stood me up, and you look like you're here alone. Interested in sharing the bottle of white wine I ordered for her?"

After a few seconds, the man responded, "Oliver Kostroma." He slid his firm, warm hand into Keith's, his callouses sliding over Keith's own palm. "I'll keep you company because you seem to be bored, but I'm not interested in white wine." Curving the left side of his lips into a half-smile, he pointed at his nearly empty bottle and added, "But you could buy me another beer."

Chuckling, Keith nodded as he picked up his menu. "Fair enough."

Before Keith could say more, the bartender arrived, carrying his bottle of wine. He smiled and nodded at the man, who introduced himself as Brendan, while pulling down a wine glass. Keith watched silently as Brendan opened his bottle and poured some into the stemware.

Keith took a sip, tasting it. He nodded his acceptance, even though the white was a bit sweeter than his normal preference. While he'd ordered it for Madeline, he would do his best to enjoy it.

"Are you interested in something off the menu, sir?" Brendan asked, placing the cork in the bottle and setting it on the bar.

Nodding, Keith told him, "I'm not interested in an entrée. I think I'll get a few appetizers to munch on." Rotating his wine glass absently, he pointed at the sampler platter. "I'll take the fried calamari, the stuffed mushrooms, and the toasted ravioli." Then Keith pointed at a different item. "I also want an order of your boneless buffalo wings."

"Good choices, sir," Brendan told him with a grin. "I'll get those started right away."

Before Brendan could take more than a step, Keith called, "And Brendan?" When the bartender turned back to him, he indicated Oliver. "And another beer for my friend, on my tab."

"Oh." The bartender glanced toward Oliver, a hint of surprise entering his expression. "Of course, sir."

Brendan quickly grabbed a bottle of the same brand as what was already in front of Oliver, popped the cap, and placed it on a fresh cocktail napkin before him. Then he hustled away.

"So," Keith began, twirling his wine glass on the bar absently. He eyed Oliver as he picked up another hot wing. "I've never sat in the bar here before."

Oliver smirked as he chewed his bite of chicken. After swallowing, he asked him, "Always here on a date?"

Keith shrugged before admitting, "Or a business meeting."

Placing the empty bone on a side plate, which contained several others, Oliver told him, "It's normally pretty quiet in here, which I like." He picked up another wing and lifted it a bit, drawing attention to his food. "Plus, the wings here are better than any others. Even those chicken wing chain restaurants that boast theirs are the best."

Watching Oliver take another bite of chicken, his lips wrapping around the meat, his even white teeth flashing as he scraped the flesh from the bone, Keith wondered what those full dark lips would look like wrapped around his cock. That thought had a predictable reaction on his dick, and he began plumping in his slacks. In fact, Keith realized he was reacting faster to Oliver than he had to all three of his last female dates combined.

Huh. How about that.

Keith had been with men in the past, although he'd never officially dated any of them. Admittedly, that had been over a decade before when he still frequented bars and clubs. If a guy caught his eye, he was happy to scratch that itch.

Good grief, man. Get it together.

Clearing his throat, Keith discreetly shifted in his seat as he took a sip of his wine. While returning the stemware to the bar, he offered, "I really enjoy their sauces, hence my ordering the boneless wings." Keith pointed at Oliver's dish. "Is it the same sauce?"

Licking his lips, Oliver used the back of one crooked forefinger to slide his plate closer to Keith. "Try the sauce."

While surprised at the brazen offer from a stranger, Keith noticed the challenge in the man's dark eyes. He smiled, refusing to back down. Reaching over, he swiped his forefinger through a dollop of the sauce that had dripped off of a wing.

Keith lifted his finger to his lips and popped it into his mouth. As he enjoyed the flavor of the rich hot sauce, he didn't miss the ever-so-slight way Oliver's eyes narrowed. His wide nostrils flared just a smidge, and heat entered his gaze for just a second before he refocused on his wings.

"Good?" Oliver asked, picking up another wing.

If Keith didn't miss his guess, Oliver's voice had deepened a bit.

Huh. Guess he's not unaffected. Wonder what those short black braids at the top of his head would feel like.

After removing every trace of the tasty wing sauce from his finger, Keith pulled it free and answered, "The same. Delicious." Allowing a smile to tease the corners of his lips, he added, "I'm just partial to using a knife and fork."

Keith wasn't a fan of having to use his hands to eat his food. He even used a knife and fork when eating a hamburger. He'd had more than a few people make fun of him for it, but he'd learned long ago how to laugh it off.

To each his own, after all.

Oliver's brows furrowed as he glanced from the wing he held between two rather messy fingers, then back to Keith. "Because you sat down next to me, I'm assuming you don't have a problem with other people using their hands."

Shaking his head, Keith stated his thought out loud. "Nope. To each his own." With a deprecating shrug of one shoulder, he added, "Just a thing with me."

"We all have quirks," Oliver answered with a nod.

As Keith took another sip of his wine, Brendan returned with his food. He hummed appreciatively as he took in the spread. His mouth watered, and he tried to decide what to try first.

The toasted ravioli. Definitely.

While Keith cut several ravioli in half, causing steam to rise from the freshly baked food, he listened to Oliver order another round of hot wings. He felt an interesting measure of pleasure upon hearing that his unexpected dinner companion wasn't hustling off just yet. Keith really wanted to know more about the handsome man sitting two stools away.

After Brendan used the open bottle of wine to refill Keith's glass, he headed toward the shifty fellow at the other end of the bar.

Keith stabbed half a ravioli with his fork and dipped it into the marinara sauce. As he lifted it to his lips, he asked, "So, Oliver. What do you do?" Then he popped the tasty morsel into his mouth, barely suppressing his groan of appreciation.

While Keith could guess that he did some kind of blue-collar work from his clothes, he wasn't about to make assumptions.

After swallowing his bite of food, Oliver picked up a napkin. "I'm an electrician," he told him, wiping his fingers clean. He swept his gaze up and down Keith's suit-clad body. With a smirk, he asked, "You a lawyer?"

Chuckling around his mouthful of food, Keith nodded. Once he'd swallowed, he told him, "I am. Senior partner of my firm." He couldn't help the pride in his voice. He'd worked damn hard to establish his firm. "Been a lawyer for over sixteen years now. Opened a firm with my friend Richard after spending a few years at one where I didn't like the politics. That was . . . twelve years ago now."

Oliver arched one black brow. "Making you over forty?"

Keith nodded. "Yep. Celebrated my fortieth over three months ago."

"Huh." Oliver tipped his head to the side a little as he swept his gaze over Keith once more in an obviously assessing way. "You look good for forty."

Grinning before taking another bite of food, Keith replied, "Thank you." He returned Oliver's open once-over, hoping his admiration for the guy showed in his eyes when he met the other man's once more. "You look pretty fantastic yourself, although I'm fairly sure you're not my age." Having always been pretty good at reading people—he had to be in his line of work—Keith guessed, "You in your early thirties?"

Oliver smirked. "I am. Thirty-one."

Damn. Almost ten years my junior.

Still, Keith had never shied away from going after what he wanted.

Curious to know more about the handsome black man beside him, Keith asked, "So, why'd you guess a lawyer? Lots of business people wear suits."

Quirking his left brow, which happened to have a small black hoop in the outer edge, Oliver waved toward Keith's body. "It's the make of the suit that sets you apart. Do you always wear *Armani* on a date? Or were you coming directly from the office?"

Scoffing softly, impressed, Keith admitted, "I was coming straight from the office." Unable to help himself, he asked, "You recognize *Armani*?"

Oliver nodded as he picked up the final wing in his bowl. "Yep. And it's a high-end one, too." He arched his pierced brow as he eyed Keith, saying, "I don't always wear steel-toed boots and jeans. I came from work, too."

"Oh, really?" Keith stabbed his fork into a piece of fried calamari and dipped it in the aioli sauce. "What do you enjoy wearing outside of work?"

"Depends on where I'm going," Oliver told him with a

grin. "But I definitely don't wear this for a date." With a shrug, he added, "Not that I think there's anything wrong with how I look."

"No, there definitely isn't," Keith replied, again giving the man an appreciative once over.

With a laugh, Oliver asked, "So, tell me about this woman who stood you up. What was up with her doing that?" Before he took a bite of his wing, he asked, "You really an asshole or something?"

Keith scoffed. "I'm sure any lawyer could be considered an asshole, but no. I don't think I am." With a shrug, he told him, "She technically called and canceled, but since it was ten minutes before she was supposed to meet me for our date, and she should have left her place well before that to be here on time . . ." Keith shrugged. "I consider it being stood up. She claimed it was because she had a headache."

"Some women," Oliver muttered, shaking his head. "Makes me glad I'm bisexual. Men are easier."

Appreciating that confirmation, Keith decided to go for it. "Well, I consider myself bisexual as well." Smiling at his impromptu dinner companion, he asked, "Can I give you a reason to dress up and take you out on a date this weekend?"

Oliver's brows shot up as his eyes widened. His surprise couldn't have been more evident. He blinked a few times, obviously processing what Keith had asked.

Finally, Oliver asked, "Are you serious?"

"I am," Keith confirmed. "I find you easy to talk to, attractive, and I want to learn more about you."

"Wow." Oliver whispered the word as he placed his uneaten wing back in his bowl. After licking his full dark lower lip, he admitted, "Been a while since someone as hot as you hit on me, let alone asked me out." Then Oliver's brows furrowed, and he shook his head. "I'm flattered. I really am, but I don't date. I swore off relationships a long time ago."

Keith felt a stab of disappointment far sharper than he'd expected upon hearing Oliver's refusal.

Huh. Odd.

It had been quite some time since Keith had been denied, and he chalked it up to that. "I'm sorry to hear that." He kept his tone light and a smile on his face. "Then I'll just settle for enjoying your company for the next little while."

"Sounds good," Oliver replied, picking up his wing again. "So, got any funny stories you can share about being in court?"

"I do." Keith accepted the change of subject in stride, burying his disappointment. "And I'll ask you in return for a funny story from your work as an electrician."

Oliver chuckled around his bite of food. "Deal."

Keith sliced a stuffed mushroom in half before taking a sip of wine, thinking about what he could tell the handsome man who'd shot him down.

Chapter Two

Hearing his phone ring, Oliver Kostroma set down the electrical cable he held in one hand. He grabbed his phone from his belt clip and stared at the number — Jimmy Gibson, although the readout of his phone read *Hot Toddy* in honor of his buddy being a bartender. With a smile, Oliver answered the call.

"Hey, Jimmy," Oliver greeted. "How are ya, man?" Grinning broadly, he forced levity he didn't feel into his voice. "How's married life treatin' ya?"

Never would he admit how damn jealous he was of his best friend. Except, Oliver knew Jimmy deserved every good thing that had come his way over the years.

Jimmy had been with his partner, Vance Weimer, for almost four years now. Technically, they weren't married, but Oliver liked to tease his buddy about it. After all, he knew it was only a matter of time. Vance had even talked to Oliver about what type of ring Jimmy would prefer.

The pair loved each other more than anything Oliver could imagine.

And that's why I'm jealous, not that I'll ever share that with Jimmy.

Snorting, Jimmy answered as he always did. "We're not married." Oliver was going to make some quip back, but then his buddy squealed into the line before saying, "But we will be soon! Vance proposed last night!"

A coil of tension entered Oliver's gut, telling him the green-eyed-monster was alive and well within him.

Shit.

Forcing the uncharitable reaction way down deep, Oliver stated, "Congratulations! I knew it was just a matter of time." He really was happy for his best friend, no matter what. "The way that man looks at you . . ." He let his voice trail off on a sigh before murmuring, "You're so damn lucky, Jimmy. Really. I'm happy for you."

"Thanks, Oliver," Jimmy said, his pleasure loud and clear in his tone. "Laramie and Trace are hosting a barbeque tonight for us in celebration. Come out and have some fun with us."

Oliver hesitated only an instant before replying, "Hell, yeah. Of course I'll be there." Grinning, he added, "You know I never miss an opportunity for free food."

Jimmy barked a laugh, and Oliver imagined his friend was rolling his eyes or shaking his head. "Yeah, you do. You've been a stranger way too often lately," he chided. "Stop distancing yourself, or I'm going to come to your house and kick your ass."

Wincing, Oliver struggled with how to respond. His buddy was right, but it was hard to hang out with all those happy, committed couples. He wanted that, but he feared what he would have to go through to get it all at the same time.

I can't open myself up like that again.

As if reading Oliver's thoughts, Jimmy murmured, "Maybe you could make a New Year's resolution to start dating again."

"No," Oliver snapped, glaring at the wall. "You know I don't date."

As he said the words, the memory of the tall, dark-haired man from the restaurant bar rose in his mind—Keith Ryzor. He'd been damn handsome and easy to talk to. When Keith had asked him out, for the first time in ages, Oliver had been oh-so-tempted.

Better this way, even if I do get lonely at times.

Before Jimmy could say more on the matter, Oliver asked, "So, what time is the barbeque tonight?"

Oliver heard Jimmy sigh, but his friend allowed him to change the subject. "Laramie is starting the grill at six-thirty, but you're welcome to come any time."

"Sounds good," Oliver stated, staring at the electrical wires he still needed to run that afternoon. "I figure I'll get done here around five, so that'll give me plenty of time to get home and cleaned up." Oliver mentally cataloged his wardrobe, trying to decide what to wear as he added, "I should be out your way before Laramie starts the grill."

Laramie Goshen ran a pig farm, although it was the cleanest operation Oliver had ever seen. He'd never even smelled anything when out there. From what Oliver had heard, Laramie had always had a nice back deck, but when Trace had moved in with him, the firefighter had helped him expand it. Now the pair enjoyed hosting barbeques with their friends on a regular basis.

While Oliver didn't really consider himself a *friend,* friend of the pair, because Jimmy lived with Vance — who was the foreman of Laramie's farm — and they were on the property, he knew that technically he was welcome there whenever.

Oliver even enjoyed the company of Vance's right-hand man, Brand. Once upon a time, Jimmy had teased Oliver about setting him up with Brand. He'd told his buddy the same thing as he'd told him now — he didn't date.

Of course, at the time, Brand hadn't even acknowledged his bisexuality. Somehow, a gray-eyed cutie — a lawyer no less — had successfully won the huge man's heart. Oliver had heard that food had been involved.

The way to a man's heart is through his stomach, after all.

The thought of food brought Oliver's thoughts back to the hottie at the restaurant bar. He'd been absolutely stunning. If they'd been standing, Oliver would bet the man stood several inches taller than himself, and his shoulders were definitely broader.

Oliver had always had a thing for bigger, broader guys. Maybe it was the way their thick arms felt wrapped around his leaner frame. Standing five-foot-ten, Oliver had what was known as a lithe runner's build.

"Oliver? You still there?"

Jimmy's voice in Oliver's ear snapped him out of his thoughts. "Yeah. Yeah," he quickly replied. After he cleared his throat, he lied, "Just thinking about this job." Oliver hoped Jimmy didn't catch him, so he quickly added, "I better get back to it if I want to get out to you on time."

"Okay." Jimmy sounded worried, and Oliver winced.

He knew his buddy would question him at the ranch, and he would have to come up with something.

"Lookin' forward to seeing you, Hot Toddy," Oliver teased with a grin. "And congrats, man. I'm really happy for you. Vance is a great guy."

So not a lie.

"Yeah. Yeah, he is." Jimmy sighed happily. "See you to-night."

"Yup. Bye, brother," Oliver stated.

After hearing Jimmy respond in kind, Oliver hung up his phone. He slid his phone into his back pocket, and doing as he always did when he started feeling a little lonely, he threw himself into work. After all, Oliver had plenty of wiring to string up before he could call it a day.

Staring at himself in the mirror, Oliver slid his hand down his chest, smoothing the form-fitting polo shirt over his torso. The dark blue fabric looked fantastic against his deep brown skin. Turning, he took in the way his black jeans cupped his ass.

Yep. Perfect.

Oliver scoffed and rolled his eyes as he turned away from the glass. "I'm not going to a club," he muttered as he took a

14

few steps away. Then he paused and peered over his shoulder at himself. "Still, it never hurts to look good, and it's a nice excuse to dress up."

With a smile on his face, Oliver headed out of his bedroom. His rented cottage had two bedrooms and one bath. He'd turned the second bedroom into a weight room, and call him vain, but he used the space religiously.

Whistling under his breath, Oliver strode through his open-concept living space. He grabbed his jacket off of one of the hooks by the door. After slipping it on, he picked up his wallet from the small table nearby and slid it into his pocket. Snagging his keys from the dish upon that same table, Oliver headed out the door.

After locking up behind him, Oliver sauntered toward his late-model *Dodge* pick-up. It sported a few dings and dents from being struck by things at work, but he kept it clean and the motor purred like a kitten—or maybe roared like a lion. He'd been asked a time or two from those he worked with on job sites as to why he didn't replace it. Oliver always shrugged and said, "It's paid for and runs great. Why mess with that?"

Oliver was always amused with the non-committal grunts or hums he received.

Once Oliver climbed behind the wheel, he pulled on his seatbelt before inserting his key and firing up the vehicle. He checked his rearview mirror before putting his truck in gear and getting underway. Absently, Oliver flipped through the channels on the radio before finding a song he liked and singing along.

The drive to Laramie's farm didn't take too long—only about thirty minutes. Oliver arrived a few minutes after six o'clock and parked in front of the large cabin Jimmy shared with Vance. Vance's son, Mark, also had a room there, but the nineteen-year-old spent most of his time at college.

Oliver had been more than impressed with Jimmy's patience when Mark had moved in with Vance full time at the age of fifteen. Evidently, Vance's ex-wife had been a homophobe and had been passing that opinion on to Mark, too. Fortunately, Mark had ended up with a crush on Lorna Lewis, the daughter of a detective with a fireman partner who she considered a second father. Lorna had helped Mark change his views.

Thank heavens.

Spotting the brilliantly lit Christmas tree in the window, Oliver figured Mark would be home on holiday. They were right in the middle of the holidays, after all. New Year's was only four days away.

Oliver turned off his truck and exited the vehicle. He didn't bother locking it after getting out. Shoving his keys into his jacket pocket, he hurried across the gravel parking area and hopped up the few steps to the deck that ran the span of the front of the cabin.

Before Oliver could even knock on the door, it was being opened. He grinned upon seeing a clearly happy Jimmy. Considering his bed-tousled light-brown hair and wide grin, giving him a just-fucked look, Oliver figured Mark was definitely not there.

"Hey!" Jimmy greeted, grabbing Oliver into a tight hug, which he happily returned.

"Hope I didn't interrupt," Oliver teased, squeezing his best friend tightly. "I could come back in five minutes or just drive right around back to Laramie's house."

Jimmy laughed while releasing him. His blue eyes twinkled as he winked at him. "Nope, we were finished," he told him, not at all shy. "Come on in."

Chuckling, Oliver followed his friend into the cabin. He spotted a bare-chested Vance coming down the hall as he slid his arms into the sleeves of a flannel shirt. The man sported a relaxed expression that could only come from great sex.

Lucky bastards.

Oliver squelched the thought just as quickly as it popped into his mind. "Good to see you again, Vance." He waggled his brows as he swept his gaze over the big man's chest. "And so much of you."

Jimmy growled as he bumped Oliver with his shoulder. "Mine. Eyes off."

Rolling said eyes, Oliver laughed. "I know Vance is yours." He turned his attention back to Jimmy. "So? Let's see the ring."

His grin back in place, Jimmy lifted his left hand. The three small diamonds embedded in the black platinum band twinkled in the light. The masculine ring looked handsome as well as serviceable.

Oliver hummed as he eyed the beautiful piece of jewelry. "It's stunning," he murmured, his gut once again twisting. Meeting his friend's gaze, he admitted, "I'm big enough to admit to being a little jealous, but I'm so very happy for you, too."

Jimmy's smile dimmed just a little, his expression taking on a hint of pensiveness. "Well, we can talk to the guys about single gay or bi men, and . . ."

"No." Oliver frowned as he snapped, "I don't need to be set up." Upon seeing Jimmy's brows furrow and his head dip—not to mention Vance's scowl—Oliver winced and quickly rested his palm on his friend's shoulder. "Sorry." Forcing a smile, he added, "Knee-jerk reaction."

"I know," Jimmy replied softly. He glanced at Vance before refocusing on Oliver and shrugging. "Guess I just want you to have the same kind of happiness I've found with Vance."

Oliver chuckled softly as he nodded. "Well, I'm good for now. Thanks." With a wink, he added, "If that ever changes, you know you'll be the first to know."

"I better be," Jimmy replied haughtily. Then his expression cleared, and he hip-checked Oliver as he walked past him.

"Give me ten minutes to finish cleaning up and putting on my make-up, and I'll be ready."

"Sure."

Oliver watched as Jimmy paused at Vance's side, getting a kiss from his man. Then he headed toward the hall that led to the bedrooms and hall bath.

Vance turned and watched Jimmy go, openly ogling his partner's ass as he went.

Biting back a snicker, Oliver headed toward the kitchen. "You mind if I grab a beer?"

"You know you never have to ask," Vance told him, turning to focus on him. He finished buttoning his flannel as he added, "Jimmy always keeps a few of your favorite on hand. He put them in the fridge after you confirmed you were coming."

Nodding, Oliver opened the fridge and grabbed a bottle. When he turned around, he noticed Vance pouring himself something from the sideboard. He figured it was vodka, recalling that was the man's drink of choice.

Oliver popped the top on his beer, leaned his hip on the kitchen bar, and brought the bottle to his lips. He took a long swig, ignoring the freeze to his throat. When he finished, he sighed and licked his lips.

Spotting Vance mirroring his pose and smirking at him with an arched brow, Oliver asked, "What?"

Vance smiled as he shook his head. "Thank you again for your help." He scoffed softly, his expression turning a bit vacant. "The expression on Jimmy's face when I got down on one knee . . . the look in his eyes . . . just wow." With a blink, Vance refocused on Oliver. "He loves the ring."

Oliver chuckled as he shook his head. "You could have asked without the ring, and he still would have looked at you like that." With a wink, he added, "But I was happy to help. I appreciate how happy you make my best friend."

Scoffing, Vance replied, "Which is why Jimmy presses you about finding a man to make you happy." With a half-shrug, he added, "Or woman. We know you're bi."

Sliding his focus to Vance's left and the cowboy-style folk art hanging on the wall, Oliver muttered, "I'm good."

Vance nodded, then took another sip of vodka. A moment later, Jimmy returned from the bedroom in form-fitting jeans and a polo shirt. His eyeliner was perfect, and his lips gleamed with gloss.

That didn't stop Vance from pecking a kiss to Jimmy's smiling lips.

Jimmy grinned at Oliver. "Ready to head over?"

Oliver chugged the rest of his beer before tossing it into the recycle bin under the counter. Turning to face the loving couple, he smiled at them. "Yeah, let's go celebrate."

Nearly an hour later, with his fourth beer in hand — Oliver had confirmed that he could sleep on Jimmy's couch — he barely kept his jaw from dropping as he watched a newcomer stride around Laramie's house and join the group on the deck.

Is that who I think it is?

The guy paused and swept his gaze over the deck. His attention snagged at the grill, and he headed that way. When he reached it, he smiled at Patrick and held out his hand. They greeted each other, but Oliver was too far away to make out what they were saying.

Oliver could have sworn the man was Keith — the guy with whom he'd shared an impromptu meal — but with the man wearing faded, relaxed-fit jeans and a crew-neck sweater, Oliver couldn't be certain.

"Who are you ogling?" Jimmy asked, relaxing onto the seat beside Oliver. He set a plate on the small table nearby and pointed at it. "That hot dog is for you. Eat it."

Glancing at the plate, Oliver took in the foot-long in the bun, which was obviously drizzled in mustard and topped with relish. "Yum," he mumbled, setting down his beer and pulling the entire small table closer to him. "These chips for me, too?"

"Yep," Jimmy quipped. "Barbeque. Your favorite." Smirking, he narrowed his eyes and pinned his attention on them. "And you didn't tell me who you were checking out."

After taking a big bite of his dog, Oliver glanced toward the deck. He couldn't help but allow his attention to linger on the dark-haired, smiling man. Oliver swallowed his mouthful, put down the dog, and picked up a couple of chips.

Tipping his chin toward the grill, Oliver silently indicated the stranger with Patrick and Laramie, who was manning the grill. "Do you know who that is?" Oliver would forever deny the way his voice grew a bit husky with admiration.

Jimmy turned and peered in the direction Oliver indicated. Narrowing his eyes, he took a few seconds to respond. Then a wide smile curved his lips as he refocused on Oliver. He even shrugged one shoulder negligently.

"I don't know him personally, but if I had to guess, that's Keith Ryzor, Patrick's partner."

Unable to help himself, a low growl escaped him. "Patrick's *partner*?"

What the hell? What about Brand?

With wide eyes, Jimmy stared at him for a heartbeat. Then he smirked. "Not *partner*, partner," he told him. "Partner as in a partner in his law firm." As soon as he quit speaking, Jimmy's brows shot up high. "Oh my god! You think he's hot!" he hissed. His blue eyes widening, he glanced Keith's way before giving Oliver a side-eyed look. "I suppose Keith is a good-looking guy. I haven't officially met him. Should we invite him over?" In the next instant, Vance joined them, and Jimmy relaxed in his seat while picking up his own hot dog. "Never mind." Before he took a bite, he muttered, "He's already on his way over."

Frowning upon seeing Jimmy's not-so-innocent expression, Oliver did his best to ignore the butterflies in his stomach.

After all, I don't date, so it doesn't matter.

Oliver wondered why his mantra of five years was beginning to be so difficult.

CHAPTER THREE

"Hey, Keith," Patrick greeted, shaking hands with him. "So glad you could make it."

"Sorry I'm late," Keith replied while releasing his co-worker's hand. "Thanks for inviting me."

In truth, until Keith had become friends with Patrick, he couldn't remember the last time he'd been invited to a barbeque. Patrick's buddies enjoyed gathering on a regular basis. When Keith had learned that Patrick used to be involved with Laramie Goshen's partner, Trace, he hadn't understood how Laramie didn't mind that Patrick was now living with Brand. It had only taken Keith seeing them all together once to understand—Laramie and Trace were just as secure in their relationship with each other, the love between them more than evident.

"No worries, Keith." Patrick chuckled as he added, "Better late than never. Besides, we all know what it's like to get hung up at work."

Keith nodded with a chagrined smile. "Isn't that the truth?"

As a fellow partner at Keith's firm, Patrick had needed to call Brand more than once to tell him that he was going to be home late.

"You ready for a burger and a beer?" Laramie offered from where he stood manning the grill. He pointed to the left. "Trace just refilled the cooler."

"Thanks," Keith replied. "That would be appreciated."

Beginning to turn, Keith swept his gaze over the group of

chatting men. He recalled most of their names, having met them at other gatherings. A black man sitting at a table off to the side caught his attention, and he froze.

Holy shit. Could it be?

"Hey," Keith murmured, tapping Patrick's upper arm with the back of his hand. "Is that Oliver Kostroma?"

Patrick peered in the direction Keith was looking. "Oh, yeah. He's Jimmy's best friend." He took the couple of steps necessary to open one of the coolers on the deck while asking, "How do you know him?"

"I met him in a restaurant bar last week," Keith told him, taking the beer that Patrick was holding out to him. "We chatted for a while." Fighting back his wince, he revealed, "I asked him on a date, but he turned me down."

Humming, Patrick nodded. "Sounds about right." He grabbed a beer for himself. "He doesn't date, or so I've heard."

"Do you know why?" Keith didn't mind pumping the other man for information.

Unfortunately, Patrick shook his head. "Afraid not. You'd have to ask Jimmy." He indicated the brown-haired man sitting next to Oliver. "He's the man of the hour, as it were. This shindig is to congratulate Jimmy and Vance on their engagement." With a grin, Patrick told him, "Vance popped the question. Heard he got down on one knee with a ring and everything."

"Wow. Good for him." After twisting off the cap on his beer, he took a sip, thinking quickly. "Well, I better go congratulate them then."

Plus, it'll be the perfect opportunity to talk to Oliver again.

Patrick smiled and nodded. "I'm gonna go whip up a plate of food. I'll talk to you later."

Keith nodded as he started toward the trio. He recognized Jimmy and Vance. They'd joined Brand on occasion when he watched Patrick in court.

Doing his best not to focus on Oliver, Keith continually glanced between the trio. He didn't want the man to know how pleased he was to see him. Considering Patrick's offhand comment, Keith also realized that asking the man out again wouldn't do him any good.

I may be an old dog, but I can learn new tricks.

Everyone needs more friends, right?

As that thought flitted in and out of Keith's mind, he realized how true it was of himself, too.

"Hey, Vance, Jimmy. I hear congratulations are in order," Keith stated by way of greeting. Smiling widely, he focused on Vance. "Patrick says you got down on one knee and everything."

"Thank you, and I certainly did." Vance grinned broadly as he turned his attention to Jimmy. He had a hand on the back of his partner's chair, and he teased his fingertips along the back of his neck. His love for his man shown clearly in his eyes. "My man was more than worth it."

Jimmy's return look was just as full of his feelings for Vance as he gazed back at him. "One of the most amazing moments of my life," he replied softly.

"May I join you?" Keith asked, indicating the empty chair nearby.

Vance's dark brow lifted, betraying his surprise. "Sure."

Keith lowered into the chair, saying, "Thanks." Finally, he acknowledged Oliver. He held out a hand, hoping the man would take it. "It's good to see you again, Oliver."

Oliver hesitated an instant before taking Keith's palm into his own. "You, too."

"I should have asked for your phone number." Keith felt the hairs on his arm stand on end upon feeling Oliver's callouses against his smoother palm. After releasing him, he relaxed back in his chair and winked at the man. "Even after you turned me down."

"Oh?" Oliver arched one black brow. "Why would you

have done that?"

Keith took a sip of his beer before answering. "You said you played racquetball, right?" One of their conversations during that meal had turned to sports they enjoyed. After seeing Oliver nod, he told him, "I do, too. It's been a while since I've played against someone new. It'd be fun."

"You play racquetball, too?" Oliver's dark eyes held just a hint of suspicion.

Keith nodded. "I do. Learned when I was fifteen." With a wide grin, he teased, "I'm pretty sure I've been playing longer than you. Lots more experience."

Oliver's eyes narrowed.

"That sounds like a challenge," Jimmy cut in. Turning his attention to Vance, he asked, "Did that sound like a challenge to you?"

"Hmmm, it really did." Vance chuckled before giving Jimmy a peck to his lips. Cuddling close to his new fiancé, he focused on Oliver. "You gonna take Keith up on his challenge?"

Taking a moment — probably to buy time — Oliver took a swig of his beer. "Why do I feel like I'm being manipulated?" he asked, his tone full of annoyance.

Chuckling, Keith answered honestly, "Because that's exactly what I'm trying to do."

Oliver lifted his chin and pinned Keith with a narrow-eyed stare. "Then why admit it?"

Keith shrugged. "I'm not going to lie to you, Oliver." Offering the other man a rakish grin, he added, "Friends don't lie to each other."

"We're friends now?" Incredulity laced Oliver's voice.

Resting his beer bottle on his thigh, Keith stared into Oliver's challenging expression. He kept his gaze level as he replied, "I'd like to be." When Oliver didn't answer right away, Keith continued, "Why do you find that so hard to believe?"

That must have been the right thing to say, for Oliver finally scoffed. His expression relaxed. He even smiled a little. "I wasn't always this paranoid," he admitted with a soft chuckle. "Yeah. Racquetball would be fun."

"Fantastic." Keith did a mental fist-pump, but he managed to keep his expression relaxed, neutrally happy. "You doing anything tomorrow morning? We can meet at the gym I'm a member at."

As Oliver took a big bite of his hot dog, he hummed. He nodded a few seconds later.

"What time works for you?" Keith pressed, wanting to make concrete plans. "Ten?"

After swallowing his bite, Oliver nodded again. "Good call on not making it too early." He used the back of his forefinger to tap the beer bottle sitting on the table. "Was planning to sleep on Jimmy's sofa tonight." Oliver curved his full lips into a smirk. "But, seein' as you want a lesson in humility, I'll switch to soda."

"Probably a good idea," Keith quipped right back. "We wouldn't want you whining about losing because you're hung over, after all."

Jimmy and Oliver laughed, while Vance snorted.

"You'll be wishin' you hadn't talked so big tomorrow," Oliver claimed before he resumed eating his food.

Keith's stomach growled, reminding him of how long it had been since he'd eaten. Lunch had been a long time ago. He glanced toward the table laden with food, hesitating. Then Keith stood.

"Phone number, Oliver?" Keith asked, pulling his own device free of his jacket pocket.

Considering Oliver had his mouth full, Jimmy answered for him, rattling off a phone number.

Keith quickly typed it into his text message app. Then he jotted a short message and pressed send. He heard a chime come from Oliver's pocket and grinned.

"Now you have mine," Keith told him with a grin while creating a new contact with Oliver's information. "I'll reserve a court and text you the address of my gym in the morning."

"Okay." Oliver smiled, his dark eyes appearing warm. "Thanks, man. It'll be fun." Then he barked a laugh as he read the text Keith had sent him — *Care to make the stakes of the game more interesting?* Smirking, Oliver typed a message back, causing Keith's phone to beep twice. Then Oliver focused on him with narrowed eyes. "If I don't talk to you later, I'll see you tomorrow."

Keith didn't want to crowd the man. He knew that would just push the guy further away from him. If Keith was to win Oliver's trust, he would need to go slow.

Keith hadn't had anyone serious in his life in a very long time, and he'd been looking to change that for years. He just hadn't found anyone worth the effort. While Keith couldn't figure out what about Oliver had snagged his attention so fully, he was never one to deny his instincts. Something told him that winning Oliver would be worth the work.

Opening the text from Oliver and reading it, Keith tipped his head back and laughed.

You're just itchin' for a beatdown. What ya got in mind, old man?

Without turning to look at Oliver, Keith smirked and tapped out a reply. As tempting as it was to make it something suggestive or sexual, he resisted the urge. He mentally reminded himself that he wasn't supposed to push the man.

The loser buys the beers at lunch afterward.

Keith focused on continuing to breathe as he waited for Oliver's response. While the man could construe his comment as angling for a date, he hoped his words about them being friends — as well as his competitiveness — would override his concern. Keith really just wanted to continue spending time with the clearly skittish man . . . get him used to his presence.

Finally, his phone beeped again. Relief flooded Keith as he read the two-word response.

You're on.

Keith smiled, tucked his phone into his pocket, and picked up a paper plate.

The following morning, after confirming a reservation for a racquetball court at his gym, Keith texted the address to Oliver. He'd spoken to the man a few more times over the course of the evening, keeping everything light and friendly. Keith had also made the rounds, talking with just about everyone, so he didn't come off as overwhelming or overbearing.

And now, I'll get him all to myself for several hours.

With his gym bag in hand and his racquet case slung over his other shoulder, Keith headed out the door. He jogged down the couple of steps that led off the porch of his crafts-man-style home and strode to the detached garage. Keith unlocked the door and headed inside.

Hitting the button on the wall beside the door, Keith caused the garage door to begin to lift. He crossed to his *BMW* and slid behind the wheel. Keith fired up his vehicle and glanced in the rearview mirror. After pulling on his seatbelt, he put the car in reverse and headed out.

"You're looking forward to this way too much," Keith mumbled to himself. "Just friends. Just friends . . . for now."

Even knowing that didn't stop him from smiling as he whistled along with the radio. Keith couldn't carry a tune in a bucket, and he knew it. However, that didn't stop him from enjoying music, mostly easy listening or soft rock.

"I wonder what kind of music Oliver enjoys?" Keith spoke aloud even as he chuckled at himself. Then he winced. "Damn. Probably stereotypical to think it, but I hope it's not rap or heavy metal shit."

Keith couldn't stand that type of music. It gave him a headache in two seconds flat. He would even be happy to tolerate country over that shit.

Pushing those thoughts from his mind—*perhaps I'll ask about it at lunch*—Keith thought about racquetball instead. He hadn't been boasting when he'd said he was pretty good at it. It had been several years since he'd lost to anyone. Most of the guys at the gym wouldn't even play with him anymore.

I'll have to go easy on Oliver. I don't want to upset him.

Still, that didn't mean Keith had any intention of throwing the game.

Just as Keith was pulling into the gym's parking lot, his phone began to ring. His car's electronic voice stated, "Incoming call from . . . Madeline Lieman."

Grimacing, Keith figured it would be rude to ignore her. He touched a button on his dash, answering the call. "Hello, Madeline. How're you doing today?" he said by way of greeting.

"I'm feeling much better today. Thank you," Madeline replied, although he hadn't actually been inquiring about her health. "Thank you for understanding about last week."

Keith parked his vehicle in a slot, leaving his *BMW* to idle. "Of course," he replied, even though he still found her actions to have been rude. "Sometimes things come up," he added diplomatically.

"Yes, they do."

While Keith waited for Madeline to get to the point of her call, he spotted Oliver climb out of a beat-up truck, a gym bag in one hand and a racquet case in the other, and start walking toward the gym door. He honked his horn while rolling down his window. When Oliver looked in his direction, Keith waved, then held up one finger, telling the man he would be a minute.

"Are you in your car?" Madeline asked.

"Yes," Keith replied honestly, watching Oliver head in his direction instead. He smiled at the handsome black man and added, "I'm headed to the gym."

"Oh." Once again, Madeline paused.

It suddenly hit Keith. Even though Madeline had called him, she expected him to ask her out again, not the other way around.

Not in this lifetime.

Keith thought quickly, trying to decide how to get off the call without being rude. "Well, I just arrived," he told her. "I'm meeting a buddy. We have reservations for a racquetball court."

By then, Oliver had stopped beside the hood of his vehicle and leaned a hip against it. He glanced at Keith for a few seconds, and Keith grimaced and held up his finger once more. Oliver dipped his head in acknowledgment, obviously realizing he was on the phone, before peering off toward the road.

"I see," Madeline commented. "I called to confirm about our rescheduled date." Finally, she stated her reason for calling. "Will you have time to get home and cleaned up from your little . . . *game* to meet me at *Delphino's* at two?"

Keith stared at the ceiling of his *BMW* for a heartbeat, praying for patience. *Delphino's* was a highly rated French restaurant—a place to see and be seen by higher society. However, if Keith went there, he wouldn't want it to be with Madeline.

"I'm sorry, Madeline," Keith responded, keeping his voice even. "But no, I won't be available." He quickly followed that up with, "And I must apologize, but I don't feel we should reschedule a date."

"You don't?" Madeline's tone definitely took on a chilly quality. "Why exactly is that, Keith?"

Keith swallowed hard, then told her, "I'm afraid my interests lie in a different direction. I'm sorry."

"Who?" Madeline demanded. "Were you cheating on me?"

Rolling his eyes, Keith reminded her, "We went on two dates, and we never agreed to be exclusive." Realizing how callous that sounded, he quickly told her, "But to answer your question, no. I didn't date anyone else during the time we were seeing each other."

"But someone else *has* caught your eye," Madeline snarked. "I should have known that a bachelor like you couldn't be trusted."

Before Keith could reply, the line disconnected. Heaving a sigh as he shook his head, he rolled up his window before shutting off his vehicle. When Keith exited his car, he spotted Oliver's wide smile.

"Hell hath no fury like a woman scorned," Keith quipped.

Oliver laughed and patted his upper arm. "No wonder you wanted to switch to guys."

Keith chuckled as he rounded to the back of his *BMW* to retrieve his gear. "Guilty as charged." Not so subtly, Keith changed the subject, saying, "Ready to get your ass handed to you?"

Snorting, Oliver replied, "You can try, but it's gonna be the other way around."

Laughing, Keith led the way to the gym.

CHAPTER FOUR

Oliver couldn't believe he'd lost. While it had been a close game, Keith had pulled out the win.

As they headed off the court, Keith bumped Oliver's shoulder with his own sweaty one and grinned at him, flashing his even white teeth. "Told ya." Then he sobered and added, "Although you're a hell of a lot better than I expected."

Scoffing, Oliver told him, "I don't know if I should take that as an insult or a compliment."

"It's a compliment," the taller man assured. He'd managed to use his height and reach to advantage a few times during the course of the game, and despite his heavier frame, Keith had been surprisingly light on his feet. "I'd like to play you again sometime. You really made me work for it."

Pinning Keith with a narrow-eyed stare, Oliver declared, "Hell, yeah, we're going to have a rematch. I'm not letting you get away with beating me by three points and that bein' the end of it."

Keith grinned. "Good. Let's go shower." With an eyebrow waggle, he claimed, "I'm ready for a beer, and I ain't buyin'."

Recalling their bet, Oliver laughed. "Yeah, yeah."

Oliver fell into step, because he knew, otherwise, he would ogle Keith's ass. The man's butt looked fantastic in his gym shorts, the silky fabric hugging his globes just right. He knew getting distracted by the man's physique had definitely contributed to his loss.

Gonna have to control that to have any hope of winning.

Still, Oliver knew that would be tough. Keith seemed to cut

a fine figure regardless of what he was wearing. In a suit, he appeared impressive. In jeans, he was gorgeous. In gym attire, Oliver found him sexy-as-fuck. He'd been fighting a semi through most of the game.

Maybe playing racquetball against Keith isn't such a good idea.

Except, Oliver knew his competitiveness would have him accepting a rematch, regardless of the consequences.

Oliver dropped back a step, allowing Keith to lead the way into the locker room. They made their way to the locker they'd chosen to share. After the bigger man opened it, Keith pulled out Oliver's duffel bag and handed it to him.

"Thanks," Oliver stated absently.

"You're welcome."

Even Keith's smile caused butterflies to dance in Oliver's gut.

Good grief.

Oliver set his bag on a nearby bench and opened it. He pulled out his towel, bathing kit, and a plastic bag. Then he began stripping out of his sweaty clothes.

Out of the corner of his eye, Oliver spotted Keith doing the exact same thing. When the larger man pulled off his top, revealing his six-pack abdominals, Oliver's mouth began to water. He really wanted to lick each dip and groove of those babies.

Oliver lost the fight with the semi, and soon he went on to full-on raging. The man was just too fine . . . and not at all shy. Keith didn't even bother turning away when he shoved his shorts and boxer briefs down his legs, revealing the curve of his hard ass as well as the healthy-sized half-hard prick.

Nearly swallowing his tongue, Oliver turned away from Keith. As swiftly as possible, he shoved off his own shorts and jockeys before wrapping his towel around his waist. Oliver knew he tented the fabric, but there wasn't a damn thing he could do about it.

After Oliver picked up his dirty clothes and shoved them

into the plastic bag, he finally gathered enough courage to turn back to Keith. Fortunately, by then, the man had his own towel slung around his waist. Oliver smiled tightly as he moved around Keith so he could shove his duffel and plastic bag back into the locker. He noticed Keith's already there as well as their racquet cases.

Oliver peered at Keith, arching one brow in silent question.

"This is a pretty high-end place, but no sense in tempting fate," Keith commented with a grin. He picked up his bathing kit and headed toward the showers.

After grabbing his own kit, Oliver followed. No other showers were in use, so they had their pick of the place. He slipped into a stall to Keith's left and closed the curtain.

Removing his towel, Oliver reached out of the stall and hung it on the hook out of the way. He placed his kit on a small corner shelf before pulling out his supplies. Then he turned on the water. Wincing, Oliver stood out of the way of the spray, but it almost instantly warmed up.

Nice!

Oliver couldn't imagine what kind of water heaters the gym had, but they must have been high-end. His skin heated as the hot water flowed over him, rinsing away his sheen of sweat. Utilizing his shampoo, he quickly scrubbed his scalp, working around the couple-inch braids that adorned the top of his head. Once he'd rinsed thoroughly, Oliver picked up his body wash and cloth.

As Oliver began washing himself, he did his best *not* to think about the fact that in the next stall over was a wet, soapy, naked Keith. Peering down at his still-bobbing cock, he knew it wasn't working too well. He grimaced as he rubbed his cloth over himself, his erection throbbing just a little, practically begging for stimulation.

Oliver stared at the drain beneath his bare feet. The sudsy water swirled around his toes before disappearing within. Unable to help himself, Oliver rested his left hand on the wall, gripped his shaft with the soft cloth, and pointed his cock toward the drain.

Then Oliver started stroking. Before he could stop it, a low moan slipped from his throat. He immediately gritted his teeth, clenching his jaw to keep in any more noises.

A few seconds later, Oliver nearly yelped in shock as a hard, wet body slid up behind his own. He peered over his shoulder as large arms slipped around his waist. One lightly tanned hand rested on his hip while the other slid around his groin, petting his pubic hair.

Meeting hunger-filled brown eyes, Oliver sucked in a sharp breath. "Keith," he whispered.

"I saw you in the same state of need, Oliver," Keith murmured huskily. At the same time, he pressed his groin to Oliver's ass, rubbing his erection along his crack. His eyes narrowed a smidge as he continued, "I'll leave, if you want me to, but I'd much rather stay" — Keith teased his fingertips over Oliver's ball sack while rubbing around the base of his erection — "and help you take care of this."

Oliver hesitated one heartbeat, two. Then the feel of Keith's fingers on his cock and balls overrode any hope for common sense.

"Yessss," Oliver snarled, bucking into Keith's hold. He dropped his cloth and placed his second hand on the wall before him. Arching, Oliver pushed back against the larger male behind him. "Get me off."

Keith's grin turned feral, and he did exactly what Oliver demanded. He began jacking Oliver's erection in swift, smooth strokes. The grip on Oliver's hip eased, giving him freedom of movement, and he smoothed that hand up Oliver's chest to tweak his nipple.

Letting out a quiet moan, Oliver shook in Keith's hold as his nipples beaded. Shudders worked through him, and his body sang as fiery tendrils of pleasure burst across his skin.

He pushed against the thick rod sliding along the sensitive skin of his crack.

Oliver focused on Keith's hand, reveling in the sensations caused by the large, tanned hand. The man alternated between stripping his dick and fondling his balls. While Oliver had at first thought the lawyer didn't have callouses, as Keith moved his palm over Oliver's oh-so-sensitive skin, he realized that wasn't accurate . . . and they felt abso-fucking-lutely exquisite.

When his balls began to tighten, Oliver muttered through gritted teeth, "Close."

"Wish I could hear your cries," Keith hissed into his ear before mouthing kisses up the tendon of Oliver's neck. With his voice still low, he added, "Wanna make you scream my name with passion."

Then Keith tightened his grip just a smidge more on Oliver's cock as he gripped and twisted one nipple.

Oliver couldn't help the soft mewl of surprise as pleasure-pain coursed through his body. Clenching his jaw, he closed his eyes as a shudder jolted through him. He couldn't fight it and wouldn't have even if he could have.

His orgasm crashed over his senses.

Sweet bliss fired through his veins as his balls forced cum up his dick in hard, ecstasy-inducing spurts. He gasped as the hairs on his arms stood on end. His stomach clenched, and he rode the endorphin high created by his release.

A low growl sounded in his ear right before heat splashed over his backside, telling Oliver that Keith had come, too. The man released his prick and settled both arms around his waist. He rubbed his cheek against Oliver's temple as he let out a long sigh, petting his abdominals with both palms.

"Damn, Oliver," Keith mumbled into his ear. "So fucking hot."

Grinning, Oliver swallowed a few times, finding his

tongue. He turned his head just a smidge, allowing him to spot Keith in his peripheral. The heavy-lidded expression on the bigger man's features caused Oliver's gut to clench for a whole new reason.

Damn. That's a good look on him.

"Yeah," Oliver conceded. "That was hot. Thanks."

Chuckling huskily, Keith lifted his head a bit and met Oliver's gaze. "My pleasure." With a wink, he began easing away from him. "And I hope we can do this again sometime."

Oliver smirked as he eyed Keith. "Racquetball? Or this?"

"Both," Keith replied, sounding relaxed and confident. Palming Oliver's ass, he gave it a squeeze. "I'll let you finish. Hurry up, though. I still want my beer." Then Keith gave Oliver's ass a smack before disappearing from his shower.

Shaking his head, Oliver muttered, "Did that just happen?" Considering he had to bend down to pick up his wash cloth, he knew that it had.

The real question was, did Oliver want it to happen again?

"Hey, how did racquetball go with Keith?" Jimmy asked, his perky voice coming through Oliver's phone.

Oliver licked his lips, trying to decide how much to tell his friend. Just that fast, he realized he would tell the man everything. After all, they always did.

They were best friends, after all.

"Well, uh, I lost," Oliver admitted. Scoffing, he added, "That hasn't happened in a while."

"Damn, really?" Jimmy whistled appreciatively. "He must be really good."

"He is. That's true," Oliver conceded. Then he bit the bullet and admitted, "Of course, I think his gym-clothes-clad body had more to do with it. The man is fucking hot in those damn nylon shorts."

Wincing, Oliver counted down in his head.

Three. Two. One.

Yup.

Right on cue, Jimmy cried, "Ollie! Are you attracted to him?" With a laugh, he quickly added, "You are. I totally knew it. You totally are. Finally!" Jimmy's pleasure came through loud and clear over the line, and Oliver could just imagine his wide smile as he continued, "Does that mean you're going to go on that date you denied him the first time?"

Oliver sighed deeply. "No, Jimmy," he countered, staring at his living room ceiling. "I don't date. You know that."

"But you like him. You're attracted to him." Then Jimmy had the audacity to add, "And you know he's attracted to you. You already told me he asked you out the first time you met."

Grimacing, Oliver sighed deeply. "We, uh . . . well—" He paused once more, knowing exactly what his friend was going to say after he admitted his next statement.

"We, uh, what?" Jimmy pressed. His tone took on a hint of suspicion. "What's going on?"

"I think we're friends with benefits."

To Oliver's surprise, Jimmy didn't yell. In fact, worry filled Oliver when the silence lengthened. He even pulled his phone away from his ear to check that he hadn't dropped the call.

When it went on too long, Oliver couldn't handle it. "Jimmy?" he mumbled. "You still there?"

"Yeah," Jimmy murmured back. "I'm here. Um." He paused once more before saying, "What do you mean by, you *think* you're friends with benefits? Wouldn't you *know* if you came to that agreement?"

Oliver could understand the man's confusion. He felt a little of it himself.

And a sounding board is just what I need right now.

"Well, after the game, we were both hard." Oliver knew he could always speak plainly to Jimmy. The man might encourage him to date, but he never judged. "Um, attraction and adrenaline. Ya know?"

"Sure," Jimmy conceded. Ever the quick-witted one, he mused, "And you guys helped each other out."

"Right," Oliver conceded. Then he admitted the confusing part. "After getting us off, Keith told me to hurry up because he wanted his free beer. We'd made a bet, you see. I paid for his beer at lunch." Oliver tried to explain before Jimmy thought it was a date. It wasn't, after all. "We ate at a chain restaurant a few doors down from the gym, and neither of us said a word about what happened."

"And Keith didn't ask you out again?"

Oliver shook his head, even though he knew Jimmy couldn't see it. "No. We talked as if we were buddies." Frowning at the ceiling, he admitted, "It was easy conversation. Light. Funny and frustrating things that have happened at work. Book and music interests. We even shared how we met all the guys and discovered we know a lot of the same people, even though we'd never run across each other until now." It had been nice—relaxing. Still, Oliver added, "Nothing too personal."

"Okaaaay." Jimmy drew the word out, then ended on a soft sigh. "Well, it sounds like Keith took you at your word. You just want to be friends, so that's what he's giving you."

"Yeah," Oliver agreed. "Yeah, it does."

So why did that make him so disappointed?

CHAPTER FIVE

K eith blew out a breath and closed the file. After attaching
it to an email, typing out a message, and hitting send, he
relaxed back in his chair. He threaded his fingers behind his
head and stretched, twisting this way and that, trying to work
out the kinks in his back and neck.

He'd definitely been sitting for too long.

Except, when Keith stood and began moving toward his
sideboard, a few twinges in his legs and arms reminded him
of a different ache. For the last four weeks, he had met Oliver
at the gym. They would play hard on the court, then release
the tension under the hot spray of the showers, sharing an orgasm in the process.

Keith loved sliding his hands over a wet, naked, soapy Oliver. The man's dark skin looked amazing under his lightly
tanned hands and felt even better. The way Oliver arched his
body, the man straining with pleasure, was absolutely mind-
bending, and his stifled cries were ball-tingling.

Everything about Oliver went to his head so damn fast that
the encounters were over far more swiftly than Keith wished.
He just couldn't seem to help himself from losing himself in
Oliver. Keith wished he could lay the sexy black man out on
his bed and explore his body for hours until they were too
sated to move.

God, I wish.

Even thinking about Oliver and their short trysts together
caused Keith's cock to plump in his slacks.

Shaking his head at himself, Keith poured himself a tumbler of whiskey and moved toward the section of his office set up as an informal meeting area. Before he had a chance to settle on one of the comfortable leather chairs, he heard a knock on his door. A glance at his clock showed him that it was just past six o'clock on Monday. Few should even still be in the office, and he knew Candice—his secretary—had left a few minutes before.

"Yes?" Keith called. When the door opened, Keith spotted Patrick. He smiled at the other lawyer and beckoned him inside. "Hey, Patrick. What are you still doing here? Something wrong?"

To Keith's surprise, Patrick stepped into the room and closed the door behind him. He inhaled deeply, his chest expanding. Shoving his hands into his pockets, he let the breath out on a soft sigh through pursed lips.

Narrowing his eyes, Keith commented, "Well, now you have me a little worried. What's up?" He motioned toward the sideboard. "Can I get you a drink?"

Patrick hesitated before nodding. "Yeah. Well, if you're willing to talk to me anyway."

"Sure," Keith immediately replied, moving back toward the drinks. He took a sip from his own tumbler, enjoying the mild burn of the high-end whiskey. After setting down his glass, he grabbed a second one. "What about? Whiskey or something else?"

Shoving his hands into his slacks pockets and rocking back on his heels, Patrick told him, "I was wondering about you and Oliver." Just as quickly, he pulled out his hands, palms out in placation. "I know it's not really any of my business, and normally I wouldn't intrude, but Brand is my partner, and he's best friends with Vance, who's marrying Jimmy"—Patrick waved his hand in the air as he rambled, and Keith was having a hard time keeping up—"and Jimmy is Oliver's best friend, and he's worried about him and—"

"Whoa, whoa." Keith waved the empty tumbler, stalling Patrick's unexpected verbal diarrhea. "I'll talk to you about it." Hell, he could use some advice. "Have a seat."

Then Keith filled the tumbler with whiskey, even though the man hadn't answered his question about it. From the guy's embarrassed flush, he figured Patrick could use it. Besides, for this conversation, Keith wouldn't mind a little liquid courage himself.

Keith picked up both drinks and returned to the lounging area. After handing off the fresh tumbler to Patrick, he took his own seat. Then he enjoyed a large sip before resting it on the leather arm.

"Okay," Keith began slowly, gathering his thoughts. "From everything you just spewed"—he couldn't help but tease a little, trying to add a little levity to the conversation— "I'm assuming that Oliver shared . . . that we've fooled around?"

That was the best way Keith could describe it. He didn't really consider giving the sexy man repeated hand jobs to be actual sex. Since they'd never said one word about what they were doing, Keith didn't know where Oliver's mind was at on the subject.

In truth, Keith had been too afraid to say anything, fearing his sort-of lover would call a halt to their shenanigans.

Patrick nodded. "Jimmy says Oliver shared, but he didn't pass on specifics to the rest of us." His cheeks took on a pinkish hue as he sipped his whiskey. With a hum, Patrick indicated the drink. "It's good."

Keith smiled a little. "I like good whiskey." Sighing, he relaxed back in his seat, crossing his left ankle over his right knee. "Do any of the other guys know you're here talking to me about this? Does Oliver?"

Grimacing, Patrick nodded. "Jimmy, Vance, Brand, and

me." His eyes widening, he quickly added, "Not Oliver. Jimmy thinks Oliver would kill us if he knew."

Offering Patrick a rueful look, Keith nodded. "You're probably right, but I wouldn't mind a little advice where he's concerned."

"Really?" Patrick pushed his black-framed glasses further up his nose. "So, you really like him?" Then his gray eyes widened. "Or you're not certain how to put a stop to it without hurting him? Because you know Vance and Brand would totally try to kick your ass if you hurt Oliver, because you'd be hurting Jimmy in the process."

"I have zero desire to hurt Oliver," Keith hurried to say. Admitting the truth, he told Patrick, "In fact, Oliver has a better chance of hurting me. I'd really like more from him, but" — spreading his free hand wide—"he doesn't date." Smirking, Keith added, "Or so he claims."

Keith took a sip of his drink, thinking of their pseudo-dates after their racquetball games. He didn't think Oliver realized what they truly were. They went somewhere alone, a pair of guys who'd just shared a sexual experience, and they enjoyed a meal together.

Most would consider that a date.

I know I do.

"What's that supposed to mean?" Patrick cocked his head.

Deciding to be frank, Keith told him. "We share texts daily." It had taken Keith a slow, careful progression to get there, but he'd done it. "We talk on the phone a couple of nights a week."

The first time Keith had called Oliver, the man had sounded so damn confused about why he would do that. He'd quickly launched into a story about seeing a guy jaywalking that day. The man had nearly been run down, and he'd been lucky that the driver had all-wheel-drive traction on his vehicle. Otherwise, he would have been slid right into on the wet and slushy roads.

Oliver had laughed and made a comment about how some people were too stupid to live.

After that, Keith always made certain he had an amusing story on hand as a reason for calling. It hadn't taken long for Oliver to start sharing stories back.

Keith continued by admitting, "We play racquetball every Saturday morning, share a dalliance in the shower while cleaning up, then go to a restaurant and get a meal together." He shrugged as he held Patrick's gaze. "To most, that could be construed as a couple building a relationship."

The more Keith had talked, the wider Patrick's gray eyes had become. His mouth even gaped.

When Keith stopped talking, he arched one brow and waited as he took a deep drink of his whiskey.

Patrick snapped his jaws shut with an audible click. After a shake of his head, he mumbled, "And Oliver has no idea that you're courting him?"

Keith smiled, pleased that Patrick understood. "No idea." Humming, he amended, "Or he's in denial about it."

After a click of his tongue, Patrick sipped his own drink. "Probably in denial," he muttered, confirming Keith's fears.

"So." Keith paused, uncertain what to say. He downed the rest of his drink and rose to get a refill. "Want more?"

Patrick shook his head. "I probably shouldn't. I'll be driving home to the farm soon."

Keith accepted that. "You're probably right." After all, he had a twenty-minute drive home, too. He sat back down and placed his tumbler on the coffee table. Resting his forearms on his knees, Keith smirked at Patrick. "So, I'm not certain how to progress with Oliver." Frowning, he asked, "Do you know why he refuses to date?"

There has to be a story there.

Shaking his head again, Patrick admitted, "Jimmy knows, but he won't talk about it." He stared into his drink as he asked, "I'm assuming you've never asked, huh?"

"No," Keith confirmed. "We don't discuss anything quite that personal."

"Why don't you start by trying to change that?" Patrick pressed softly. "And in the meantime, I'll talk with the guys and see what we can come up with to, uh . . . help."

Keith smiled as he nodded. "Thanks. You and the guys' support means a lot to me." It did, too. If anyone could help, it was Oliver's best friend and those associated with him. After all, they were Oliver's true family.

He'd asked Oliver about his upbringing once, but the man had just shrugged and told him, "Only child. Dad died when I was seventeen, right after I was accepted for an electrician apprenticeship. Made him proud." For just an instant, he smiled. His features cleared as he scoffed and added, "Mom married Dad's *best friend* within three months." He made air quotes. "I think they were having an affair." Oliver sported a dark expression for one heartbeat, then two, before he pinned a forced-looking smile on his face and focused on Keith once more. "Anyway, I got my own place, and they moved to Florida. We don't talk. I've been on my own ever since."

Keith hadn't known how to respond. While his family wasn't all roses and sunshine, his teenage and young adult years were far better than Oliver's unspoken of rough ones. His parents were wealthy—descendants of one of the first families to put in a vineyard in the southern Oregon valley. His college and post-graduate courses had all been paid for.

While Keith's mother harped on him for still being unwed—and he knew she was going to blow a gasket if he ever convinced Oliver to make what they had official—they'd always supported him . . . eventually.

Fortunately, Keith's younger sister, Trudy, had an amazing head for wine, and she was already making their family legacy even more popular.

"Thank you again," Keith stated, his tone heartfelt, as he

again rose, this time when Patrick did. "I enjoy my time with Oliver, find him hot as hell, and want to see where a relationship with him could go." Knowing he'd already said all that, he still added, "I just can't figure out how to get past his defenses."

Patrick reached over and patted his upper arm. "You've got friends in your corner." Then he scowled as he narrowed his eyes. "Of course, that also means there are plenty of people to bust your chops if this goes sideways."

Barking a laugh, Keith lifted his hands in placation. "Got it. Don't hurt Oliver." Sobering, he told his co-worker and friend, "I sure as hell don't want to. I'd love to see what we could have together." Moving toward his desk, Keith began buttoning his suit coat, readying to snag his outer coat to pull over it. "I just want a chance."

Heading toward the door, Patrick told him, "It sounds like you've already made fantastic inroads. I'll talk to the others and get back to you."

"Thank you, again." Keith appreciated the support. As he watched Patrick wave and open his office door, he offered, "Have a safe drive home and a great night."

"You, too." Then Patrick was gone.

Keith grabbed his briefcase and hurried to follow his example.

Refilling his wine glass after supper, Keith contemplated going to his home office and doing a bit more work. He knew he had very little life, but he was also getting better at it. Over the last couple of years, he'd begun to expand his circle of friends and activities. Keith knew he didn't get to nearly as many barbeques and events as the guys invited him to, but he was making progress.

Still, sitting at home alone on a weeknight, he often found himself turning to work just to fill the time.

Either that or working out in his basement home gym, but he wasn't feeling that ambitious that evening.

Sighing deeply, Keith headed to the office. He'd just reached the door when he heard his phone ring. For just an instant, hope flared through him, thinking it was Oliver calling him for a change.

A look at his screen filled Keith with a different sort of hope. After all, he couldn't think of a reason Jimmy would call within just a few hours of his talk with Patrick. Maybe the man had some advice.

"Hi, Jimmy," Keith greeted, continuing to his office. "How are you this evening?"

"I'm sorry to bother you on a Monday night, but I'm hoping you can help."

Not liking the stress bleeding through Jimmy's voice, Keith instantly replied, "Of course." He placed his wine glass on his desk and rested his empty hand on his hip. "What's going on? Is it Oliver?"

Keith couldn't imagine why else Jimmy would be calling him. After all, Patrick handled Jimmy and Vance's custody paperwork of Vance's son, Mark.

"It's Oliver. He needs help," Jimmy told him, cementing his fears. "I just got a call from Clayton. He's another bartender at The Red Door where I work." Jimmy spoke swiftly, his concern clear. "Evidently, Oliver is there, and from the way he's acting, Clayton is worried someone roofied him. He's only had two beers, and he's acting really out of it." Fear bled into Jimmy's voice as he continued, "Some guy already tried to help Oliver off his barstool, but Clayton put a stop to it. I'm almost forty minutes away, and you're—"

"Only ten," Keith cut in. Halfway through Jimmy's explanation, he'd already started striding swiftly through his craftsman. "I'm leaving now. I'll call you when I get there."

"Thank you," Jimmy replied, his relief clear. "God, if something happens to him because of me, I'd never forgive myself."

Keith yanked his coat halfway on and grabbed his keys all while stuffing his feet into a pair of loafers by the door. "I'm certain whatever happened"—he paused to shift the phone into his other hand, allowing him to slide his second arm into his coat sleeve—"the only one at fault is the guy who administered the roofie." With a growl, Keith added, "And if I figure out who that is, I'll make them pay."

"We all will," Jimmy countered as Keith jogged out of his house and headed to his detached garage. "But I normally work Monday nights, and I forgot to tell Oliver I managed to snag the night off. I—"

"Again, still not your fault," Keith snapped. "I'm in the car. I'll call you back shortly."

"Okay."

Keith disconnected the call, fired up his *BMW*, and headed to the bar. It had been some time since he'd been to The Red Door—probably over three years—but he recalled the location. Barely taking his foot off the accelerator, Keith made it in record time.

Shutting off his vehicle while sliding from his seat, Keith almost hung himself on his seatbelt. He cursed under his breath as he released it, then jogged toward the bar. Entering, Keith garnered a questioning look from the bouncer, but he didn't say anything.

It was about that time that Keith figured what he must look like. He still had on his expensive suit slacks, but he'd stripped his torso to his white wife-beater. Over that, he wore a high-end, calf-length overcoat and finished off his look with comfortable house shoes.

Oh well.

Keith paid the cover charge and headed inside, making a beeline for the bar. Spotting a large man slinging drinks and looking worried, he pegged him for Clayton. He'd probably been introduced to him a couple of times, but he doubted the guy recognized him. Instead, Clayton appeared far too busy searching the area even as he created some mixed drink.

"Clayton," Keith called, catching his attention. Once the man turned a frown his way, he stated, "Jimmy called me. Where's Oliver?"

A quick scan of the bar told him that his love-interest wasn't within sight.

"I don't know," Clayton replied, his expression once again returning to worried. "He was here a couple of minutes ago, but I got busy and lost track of him."

Growling under his breath, Keith swept his gaze over the area again. Being a club, it wasn't as if it was extremely well lit. People moved in waves on the dance floor, obscuring most features. The people at the tables huddled together, talking and flirting over their drinks.

Just as his concern caused his gut to clench, a familiar set of black braids caught Keith's attention. He squinted, making out Oliver's head on some blond-haired guy's shoulder. The man had a thick arm around Oliver's waist and was practically carrying him past the last table toward the exit.

"Spotted him," Keith snarled.

Then Keith began shoving through the other patrons, his only focus on reaching Oliver.

Chapter Six

Oliver's head swam. His gut clenched. Even his vision blurred. He heard the laughter and chatter of men as well as the sound of music blaring, but he couldn't seem to focus on anything.

"Come on, buddy," a deep voice urged. "One foot in front of the other."

Not recognizing the voice, Oliver tried to lift his head, but all that did was make his senses swim even more. He groaned and tried to double over. Except, someone was holding him upright while forcing him to keep walking, regardless of how uncoordinated he moved.

"Hey, is he all right?"

Wait. I know that voice. Blain, the bouncer at the door.

"Oh, yeah," the stranger replied, good humor lacing his words. "Just had one too many. Gonna pour him into bed so he can sleep it off."

"Make sure Oliver has plenty of fluids," Blain ordered, his concern clear. "Or he won't like how he feels in the morning."

When the man helping him spoke, to Oliver's thinking, he sounded just a little sinister. "Don't worry. I'll make sure Oliver is just fine."

Who the fuck has me?

Before Oliver could manage to get his tongue to do more than slur Blain's name, the stranger was forcing him to move again.

Fuck!

Oliver knew what it felt like to have a few too many drinks, and this wasn't it. Something was wrong. He just wished he could stand still long enough to figure out what it was.

Unfortunately, the guy wouldn't allow him to stop and get his bearings.

The fresh air should have helped, but it didn't. His senses still reeled. His tongue felt three times its normal size. Even his throat felt dry, as if he'd chugged sand.

God. What's going on?

"Oh, you are going to feel so good wrapped around my cock." The man's voice crooned into his ear. "Oliver, is it?" He chuckled coldly. "Mmmm, I love it when I know what name to put on a picture. It makes the memory that much sweeter."

What the ever-loving hell?

"I know you can still hear me, Oliver," the asshole continued. "The drug I used didn't knock you out completely. That would be no fun."

Suddenly, Oliver found his back leaning against a car. A tight hand on his chin forced him to lift his head. Through blurry vision, Oliver saw blond hair, blue eyes, and fair skin. His attention ended up snagged on the man's mouth and the gap caused by a missing tooth, stained teeth, and — *holy hell* — his eyes began to water even more from the stench of the man's breath.

Revolting.

Oliver tried to lift his arms, to push the man away, but it felt as if heavy weights were attached to his wrists. Even mustering up the energy to turn his head seemed too great an effort. Disgust coiled in Oliver's gut as he watched the man's face descend.

"Oliver!"

Relief upon hearing Keith's deep voice flooded every fiber of Oliver's being. If he'd been able to get his tongue to work, he would have cried out with joy. Instead, he could do nothing but lean against the side of the car, and he wouldn't even have been able to do that if the man he realized was intending to assault him hadn't had a hand clamped on his hip.

Instead, bile rose up his throat. He tried to swallow it, but he couldn't manage to with whatever drug was ravaging his system. Choking, the burning fluid dribbled past his lips and down his chin.

Oh, god.

Tears threatened, stinging the corners of his eyes. Never in a million years would he want anyone to see him like this, least of all Keith. As much as Oliver knew he needed the man's help, he wished his savior could be anyone but him.

"Oliver, just breathe, buddy." Keith sounded angry even as he attempted to soothe Oliver. "I got him now. Step back."

Oliver's attacker sneered. "Get lost, man. My boyfriend just had a little too much to drink. I got this."

Keith's deep voice took on a commanding edge. "Oliver is *not* your boyfriend, and if you don't release him, I'm calling the cops." Then a hardness filled his tone, and Oliver wondered if that was how he sounded in court. "In fact, I think I should call them anyway. Have you put in holding. We'll see if Oliver recognizes you when he —"

He found it hot and scary all at the same time, and he was having a hard time focusing on Keith's actual words.

"Whatever, man," his attacker snarled. "You deal with Oliver's drunk ass."

Then the guy's hand on Oliver's hip disappeared, and he began sliding down the car, his legs unable to bear his weight.

"I'll see you later, Ollie baby," the guy called, his voice sounding low and mean even as it grew fainter. "When you don't have your friend around."

"Easy, Oliver," Keith rumbled, catching him before he hit the ground. "Just focus on breathing," he encouraged. "Let's get you out of the cold."

With Keith's words, Oliver realized that he was indeed cold. In fact, in a sort of *out-of-body experience* way, he even recognized that he was shaking. Then, to Oliver's amazement, Keith eased an arm under his legs and lifted him, cradling him to his chest.

For the first time since his senses became discombobulated, Oliver felt as if he could breathe, could relax. He knew, deep down in his soul, that he was safe with Keith. Relaxing against the larger man carrying him, he focused on nothing but taking his next breath.

Even his swimming senses were no longer a concern.

Keith would take care of everything.

"I'm going to lay you in the back seat of my car, Oliver," Keith crooned into his ear. "Just relax now." A second later, he heard Keith grumble, "Damn it. I don't even know if you can hear me. God, I want to take that fucker apart so bad."

Blinking several times, Oliver forced his head to tip up just a little. That allowed him to peer into Keith's handsome features. He spotted the stress lines creasing Keith's frowning features and wished he had some way to ease them. Except, when Oliver opened his mouth, he couldn't manage to force anything out.

Keith must have spotted the movement, for he smiled down at him. "Hey, handsome." His gaze roved over Oliver's features as he continued, "If you can hear me, blink once, nice and slow."

Oliver slowly did as he'd been told, ignoring the effort that even that action took.

"Okay, good. Very good." Keith's smile took on an obvious edge of relief. "You have a number of people worried about you."

While Oliver tried to smile, to offer even that bit of reassurance, he couldn't seem to do it.

"You just relax here, Oliver," Keith ordered, carefully using the arm under Oliver's knees to open the back door of his sedan. "I'm going to call for an ambulance."

Upon hearing that, Oliver managed to gather a bit of strength. He couldn't stop Keith from placing him in his back seat, but he managed to snag his fingers on his jacket as he drew away. Grunting more than speaking, he did his best to object.

Oliver didn't want anyone to see him like this. He just wanted to go home and forget the whole experience. Never in his life had he felt so helpless, and he hated it.

Perhaps it was part of being a lawyer, but Keith seemed to read his responses. "You don't want to go to the hospital?"

With great effort, Oliver managed to shake his head once.

Keith sighed deeply. His jaw clenched. "I don't agree with your decision," he whispered, his voice rough. "But I'll respect it." Sliding his fingertips along Oliver's braids, Keith added, "But I'm not leaving you alone tonight either, so don't even try to ask."

Then, to Oliver's surprise, Keith bent and pressed a kiss to his forehead. "Rest while I drive," Keith ordered before easing away, out of the car, and straightening.

Oliver could do little else as Keith closed the door and climbed behind the wheel. After the car started moving, Keith stated, "Call Jimmy."

The call was answered within half a ring.

"Did you find Oliver? Is he okay? What happened? Clayton said you went tearing out of the place."

"I spotted Oliver being half carried, half dragged from the club," Keith stated bluntly. "He's clearly been incapacitated with something. I stopped the asshole from taking him. Got a picture of him, too. And the license plate number of the car he tore ass out of the parking lot in."

Jimmy growled before asking, "What hospital are you taking him to?"

Keith sighed heavily. "Oliver doesn't want to go to a hospital."

"So he's talking?" A heartbeat later, Jimmy demanded, "And why the hell not? What if there are lasting effects to whatever that dirtball gave him?"

"I imagine he's embarrassed," Keith replied, his tone soft and full of understanding. "And he's not speaking per se, but he is aware."

"Can't speak and you're not taking him to the hospital?" Jimmy shrieked through the line. "What the hell, Keith?"

"I'm respecting his wishes, Jimmy," Keith stated gruffly, frustration filling his own tone. "But I will be placing a call to Carl."

"Then I'll contact Randy," Jimmy immediately replied, followed by, "Vance, call Randy."

Oliver tried to growl, knowing exactly who they were referring to. Carl Lewis was a detective and a friend of the group. His partner was a firefighter by the name of Vincent Androse. Whenever the group had a problem, Carl and his detective partner, Ryan Straton, were the first people they contacted. Randy Coughlan was a paramedic in their circle of friends, and he'd often helped out a pal in need of a bit of first aid.

Except, Oliver didn't need his stupidity aired out in front of his friends.

"Hmmm, it seems Oliver is improving," Keith commented mildly. "He's glaring at me."

Huh. I am glaring. That's improvement. Go figure.

Stopping the car, probably for a red light, Keith turned in his seat so he could focus his full attention on Oliver. "I don't care if you end up pissed at me for this," he told him, his brown eyes gleaming with concern as he stared at him. "The cops need to be notified, and you know our friends are discreet."

Oliver wanted to snap, "Not if I have to testify." Except, he couldn't make his mouth work.

55

"Consider this," Keith continued, his voice soothing and cajoling all at the same time. "That man is brazen enough to walk into a bar, drug you, and ignore a watchful bartender to whisk you out of there to do god knows what."

I don't want to think about what he was going to do.

Keith kept talking. "That means he's confident. He's experienced." His tone took on an even more serious quality. "Oliver, he's done this before. Perhaps many times." Keith paused, perhaps for effect. "That man must be stopped."

Oliver closed his eyes. He didn't want to see Keith's serious expression anymore. He didn't want to see the encouragement and determination within the man's brown orbs.

The honk of a car horn heralded the vehicle moving forward once more.

Blinking back tears of frustration, Oliver stared at the ceiling of the vehicle as Keith made his way down one road and up another. He couldn't have guessed how long the ride was, but it felt like an eternity. That was most likely due to the fact that he could barely move.

Finally, Keith's car stopped, and the engine grew silent. The front door opened, then closed. For just an instant, he found himself alone, and fear stabbed through his chest. It once again started getting hard to breathe, as if a weight settled over him.

A second later, the door near his head opened. "Hey. Easy, Oliver." Keith knelt near his head and gently rubbed his fingertips along his hairline. "You're okay. I won't be far until you get your mobility back," Keith promised, obviously recognizing his feeling of insecurity. Holding Oliver's gaze, he told him, "I need to go open the front door. Then I'll be right back. Less than ten seconds."

With some effort, Oliver swallowed, trying to ignore the nasty taste still in the back of his throat. Then he managed to nod.

Keith skimmed the backs of his forefingers along his jaw as

he nodded. "Okay. Be right back."

Then Keith was gone, and Oliver wished he could call him back . . . but his voice still couldn't work.

As if somehow reading his mind, Keith started talking, letting him know what was going on. "I'm climbing the five stairs to my craftsman." That was followed by a couple of soft thuds, probably because the big man was taking them two at a time. "Did you know I've been living here for almost twelve years?" Keith chuckled as he continued, "Unlocking the door. There we go." The sound of him turning reached Oliver's ears, and the way Keith's voice began to grow louder told him that he was on his way back. "This house was built almost eighty years ago. When I bought it, it was a steal." His face appeared in Oliver's line of sight, a small smile curving his lips as pleasure lit his brown eyes. "I doubt you'll believe me, but I did most of the restoration myself. I did use trades for electrical and plumbing, though." After winking at him, Keith shocked him again as he bent and pressed a kiss to his temple. "After you get well, maybe you'll want to take a look at my wiring. Tell me if I hired a good contractor. Alright. I'm going to lift you now. Come on, baby."

Oliver appreciated Keith's attempt to create levity. He didn't know whether to focus on the man's occasional term of endearment or the fact that he intended to get the police involved. His mind spun with everything that had happened to him in the last hour, and he couldn't seem to focus on anything.

Or maybe that's still the drugs in my system.

Fuck. I hate drugs.

Even the time Oliver had dislocated his shoulder falling off of a ladder while running electrical wire, he hadn't even filled his prescription. He'd gotten by on over-the-counter medication or through meditation exercises. After that, he'd started taking tai chi.

Too bad that didn't help me stop from getting drugged.

CHAPTER SEVEN

K eith hated the lost look on Oliver's usually strong and vibrant features. He wished he could take it all away from him. Due to the fact that he couldn't, Keith vowed to help the man through it in any way that he could.

To that end, Keith kept on talking. He chatted about anything that popped into his head, from the number of times he'd had to sand the porch to the number of boards he'd had to replace. He hoped it gave Oliver something to think about other than what he was going through. Once he was in the house, he used a foot to kick his door closed.

Taking Oliver through his foyer and into his living room, Keith carefully placed him on his sofa. He grabbed the throw blanket he kept across the back and spread it over Oliver's body. Then Keith touched his temple before pointing to the left.

"My kitchen is through that doorway. I'll be right back."

As Keith moved away, he pulled his phone back out of his pocket and dialed Carl Lewis's number. When he received no answer, he tried Ryan Straton. To his relief, the man picked up on the second ring.

"This is Straton."

"Detective Straton, this is Keith Ryzor," Keith said by way of greeting. "Thank you for answering."

"Keith?" The man sounded confused for just an instant before he repeated Keith's name, recognition in his tone. "Keith Ryzor." Keith wasn't surprised, considering he'd only spoken to the detective in passing. "What can I do for you?"

"I need to report an assault to one of our friends." Keith started the water running on the hot setting before grabbing a dish towel from a drawer. "Oliver was drugged this evening at The Red Door. Jimmy said he was contacting Randy, so he should be on his way over to check him."

"Damn," Ryan growled. "Gotta go, babe. I'll try not to be long." Then the unmistakable sound of someone kissing another came through the line. A second later, Ryan returned to the line. "Is Oliver still at the bar? Or is he on the way to a hospital?"

Grimacing, Keith admitted, "Oliver didn't want to stay there." As he soaked the towel in warm water, he told the detective, "Randy is coming in as a friend."

Ryan grunted. "Got it. Kid gloves." Then he asked, "Where is he?"

"At my place. With me."

There was a few seconds of silence followed by the unmistakable deep-squeak of a vehicle's door hinge. "Okay. Where are you at, Keith?"

Keith turned off the water before rattling off his address. At the same time, he wrung out the dish cloth.

After another few seconds of silence, Ryan told him, "I'll be there in fifteen."

"Thank you, Detective."

Scoffing, Ryan muttered, "Better just be ready to do plenty of groveling to your man."

"I wish," Keith whispered, but the line had already gone dead. Sighing, he shoved the phone into his pocket before heading back to his living room. "Hey, Oliver," Keith murmured. "I'm walking up behind you, babe." Before he rounded the sofa, he grimaced.

Shit. That just keeps coming out. These damn protective instincts flooding me are making controlling my tongue so damn tough.

Clearing his features, Keith rounded the sofa and dropped to one knee. "I'm sorry," he began softly, hating the fact that

Oliver wasn't making quips back at him. "I should have turned the TV on for you." Gently, Keith wiped the traces of spittle from the man's goatee and chin. "I really want to give you some water, but I'm worried to until you've been cleared by Randy." Offering Oliver his most beseeching look, Keith murmured, "Just hang on a little longer. Okay?" An idea coming to him, Keith found a clean corner of the wet cloth and held it up. "Open your mouth. I'll wipe your tongue. It's not water, but it's something."

Even as Oliver opened his mouth so Keith could do as he'd offered, he peered into Oliver's dark brown eyes and saw the frustration within their depths. His heart went out to this amazing man, and he barely resisted the urge to take the man's lips with his own. In all the fun showers they'd shared, they'd never been that intimate, and Keith didn't think Oliver would appreciate it now.

Talk about a breach of trust.

After soaking Oliver's tongue and washing away all the spit-up he'd choked out in the parking lot, Keith set the cloth aside. He tucked the blanket even tighter around him, then grabbed the remote off the coffee table. Finally, he flipped on the TV, keeping it at a low volume.

Keith settled next to Oliver and curled his arm around him. Rubbing his opposite shoulder and up the side of his neck, he whispered, "You once told me you loved watching *Survivor* with Jimmy. Can I put a favorite season on for you?"

To facilitate that, Keith pulled up video-on-demand on Amazon. He would be happy to buy whatever season the man wanted if it would make him happy. After doing a general search under TV programs and locating all seasons available for download, Keith refocused on Oliver.

Seeing the question in Oliver's dark eyes, Keith tried to decide what the man was asking. He could only guess, so he hoped he got it right.

"No, I've never actually seen the reality show." With a half-shrug and a grimace, Keith admitted, "I've seen a commercial or two, but in case you haven't noticed, I'm a bit of a workaholic." Offering a chagrined smile, he ducked close and whispered, "I'd love to find some show to while-away the hours with you. Think you could share *Survivor* with me?"

To Keith's relief, a new light appeared to gleam in Oliver's eyes, and the corners of his lips twitched.

I'll take it.

Just as swiftly, another thought struck Keith.

God, I hope this show doesn't suck.

Of course, Keith knew that even if he did decide he didn't like the show, he would never admit it. If doing this with Oliver made the man happy, relaxed — and helped them connect — he would deal with it.

"So, what do you think, then?" Keith teased with a wink. "Where should I start?"

Even with only the corners of Oliver's lips twitching just a smidge, Keith could guess at the man's thoughts. He grinned. "As near to the beginning as I can?"

To Keith's pleasure, Oliver offered one slow blink — meaning yes.

"Alright." Keith took it as a challenge. "Let's see the earliest season they have available."

Keith began to scroll.

After a few seconds, Keith hummed and said, "Oh, look. Season One." He focused on Oliver and waggled his brows. "Shall I start it?"

Once again, a bit of warmth lit up Oliver's eyes from within.

"Then let's do it."

Keith hit the *Buy* button. For a few seconds, he watched the processing symbol on the screen. Then it flicked off, and he was taken to the first episode.

Lifting the remote, Keith prepared to push play . . . when a knock on the door interrupted him.

Turning his attention back to Oliver, Keith saw the haunted look had returned to his face, and he barely managed to bite back a growl. Instead of cussing, he assured, "We'll return to this as soon as we clear everyone out of here." He spotted the sadness and embarrassment in Oliver's eyes, the way he opened and closed his mouth, even though no sound came out. Hating that, Keith pecked a kiss to Oliver's temple once more and whispered the reminder, "These are our friends, and they're here to help."

Oliver gave an almost imperceptible nod, and Keith took it.

After touching Oliver's goatee once more, Keith rose from his seat and headed to the front door. He could practically feel the man's gaze boring into his back. Pausing in the archway that led to the foyer, Keith turned and smiled at Oliver before dipping his chin in a nod.

The knock had started again, followed by the ring of his bell.

Keith checked through the peep hole before opening his front door. He found Randy standing there, holding a bag in one hand, and Ryan was just pulling up. After waving at the detective, Keith left his door open before leading Randy into his home.

"Randy's here, Oliver," Keith called, since he couldn't see them. "Ryan is about thirty seconds behind him, just pulling up."

Heading back around the wall to enter the living room, Keith saw Oliver's gaze sweeping over them, clearly searching.

Smiling at Oliver, Keith crossed to his side. He touched his shoulder in encouragement before refocusing on Randy. The younger man had been a paramedic for over ten years, and he was damn good at his job. Keith trusted him to help.

"Hey, Oliver," Randy greeted softly, his brows furrowing

deeply as he roved his gaze over him. "I hear some asshole decided to cause problems with you." Lowering to one knee a few inches from Oliver's prone form, Randy placed his bag on the sofa beside him. "Let's see what I can do to make you feel better."

Keith hoped that was a lot.

"I can see you're with us, Oliver," Randy continued as he peered into his eyes, his voice soft. He gently began unwrapping the blanket from around his shoulders. "Do you have much mobility?"

Oliver's body seemed to flinch, just a smidge, as if he were fighting with himself.

"Hey, it's okay," Keith dropped to his knees. He heard the front door close, but he ignored it. Resting his right palm on Oliver's thigh, he murmured, "It'll come back to you. Don't fight it, yet. You're safe here." Turning his attention to Randy, Keith grumbled, "That answer enough?"

Randy fixed a pained smile on his face. "Yeah, but it's my job to check." Turning his focus to his bag, he began pulling supplies from the satchel. "Is there anywhere that Oliver was hurt?" Randy glanced at Keith, telling him he directed the question at him.

Keith focused on Oliver for a few seconds, reading his eyes. Then he shook his head. "Not that he's aware of." With relief filling him, he glanced Ryan's way so he knew the detective spoke to him, too. "Clayton, the bartender at The Red Door, noticed something was off, so he stopped the asshole from moving Oliver from his seat the first time. Then he called Jimmy." Keith smiled at Oliver. "He knows you're best friends, and Jimmy called me because I'm only a few minutes away."

Oliver had clear questions in his eyes, and Keith could guess at what some of them were — like, why would he drop everything to help him?

While Keith intended to have that conversation with Oliver — probably sooner rather than later, due to this incident — he had no intention of bringing it up right at that second. Instead, he continued to share what he knew of Oliver's attack.

"When I arrived, a rush of customers gave some blond asshole a chance to sneak Oliver away from Clayton." Grimacing, Keith admitted, "I was so focused on getting to the bar, I didn't notice the bastard slipping him around the outside of the seating area of the club. I had to play catch-up, which I did in the parking lot." Keith pulled his cell phone from his slacks and opened his gallery. "I took his picture, and I can tell you the license plate of the car he drove away in."

Keith held out his phone to the detective.

"Okay, Oliver," Randy murmured, easing his arm out from beneath his blanket. "I'm going to draw some blood so we can determine what you were drugged with." He arched one brow as he looked Keith's way for a second. "If Oliver needs more than fluids and time, we need to know about it."

After a squeeze to Oliver's knee as well as a reassuring smile, Keith gruffly ordered, "Go ahead." He held Oliver's focus, touching his chin and holding his attention as Randy slipped the needle into his love-interest's arm. "You'll be fine, babe," he murmured, unable to help himself. "We'll get you fixed up, and we're going to nail this bastard so he can never do this to you or anyone else again."

Oliver swallowed so hard his Adam's apple bobbed, but he continued to stare back at Keith until Randy softly murmured that he was finished.

"I'll get this analyzed as swiftly as I can," Randy assured while wrapping a bit of gauze around Oliver's arm. "For now, rest, fluids, broth or soup. Between the beer and drugs, he needs to get hydrated." He focused on Keith, questions in his eyes. "Me or one of the guys will bring you some supplies if you don't have any." Before Keith could remember what he had in his cupboards, Randy continued, "Oliver should be monitored for the next forty-eight hours, and me or Wade should be called with any problems." Randy referred to his fellow paramedic. "Do we need to set up a schedule?"

Keith immediately shook his head. "Nope, I'll be here," he stated firmly. "I'll take care of everything."

"Even undressing him and taking him to the bathroom?" Randy challenged. "There's no telling how long this shit is going to immobilize him."

Fighting against the tick in his jaw caused by someone questioning that he would take care of his man—*somehow, I'll make him mine by the end of this*—Keith simply nodded. "If Oliver feels the need, he'll find a way to let me know, and we'll handle it."

Randy eyed him for a long moment before nodding slowly. "Okay." He held out his card. "My cell is on the back in case you need me."

Keith took it and placed it on an end table. "Thank you."

"Here's your cell phone back." Ryan held out his phone. "I'm also going to need the rest of the story." He cocked his head as he scowled at Oliver. "We'll find this bastard, Oliver," the detective claimed, a growl in his voice. "Don't you worry. We're gonna make this asshole pay."

Even though Keith knew that wasn't what Oliver wanted in that exact moment—hell, he figured the man just wanted to be left alone and forget that this had ever happened—he still nodded. "Good."

Then Keith shifted his attention to Randy, who was rising to his feet. "My kitchen is through there." He pointed. "Can you rummage through my fridge and let me know which juice would be okay along with water?" Keith enjoyed several flavors, so he hoped Oliver could have a couple of them. After Randy nodded and headed deeper into his home, Keith focused on Ryan and told how he'd extricated Oliver from his attacker.

Less than twenty minutes later, Keith saw Randy and Ryan out of his home. He returned to his living room. Instead of making a big thing of what had just gone down, he decided to focus on relaxing Oliver.

Settling on the sofa beside Oliver, Keith once again tucked the blanket around the man. He offered him a drink of water, helping him with the straw. After placing the cup on the coffee table, he picked up the remote.

"Okay," Keith started, cuddling Oliver to his chest. "Let's check out this *Survivor* that you love so much."

It didn't matter if the show was the worst in the world. Keith would sit there, helping the man relax until he felt normal again.

CHAPTER EIGHT

Oliver wasn't entirely certain how many episodes of *Survivor* they'd watched before he'd drifted off, but he was pretty sure they were somewhere halfway through season two.

Wow. Keith looks fantastic when he laughs.

Over the course of watching the show, Oliver had seen Keith laugh so many times. He couldn't believe how much the man actually enjoyed the reality show. Oliver had never had a guy he'd dated enjoy the show, let alone be the one willing to watch episode after episode with him.

While Oliver understood that Keith was probably doing this to keep him company while he was incapacitated, he realized it was still the nicest thing any of his boyfriends had ever done for him . . . combined.

Except, he's not really my boyfriend, is he?

All those thoughts flitted through Oliver's mind before he even tried to open his eyes.

Oliver slowly blinked open his eyelids and peered around the area. He recognized Keith's living room. The TV screen still showed the screen for *Survivor*, waiting for Keith to approve the start of the next episode.

Damn. He's already started season three. Huh.

In truth, Oliver would love *Survivor* fests to help Keith catch up on his favorite reality TV show. He figured there were some episodes he hadn't seen, either. The show had been on for over twenty years, after all, typically putting out two shows a year. That was a *lot* of episodes.

The next thing that hit Oliver was that he was sprawled over Keith's chest. At some point, Keith must have moved them, laying them both down on the cushions of the massive sectional. Oliver's head rested on Keith's chest, and his lower half was cradled between Keith's powerful legs. He'd spread the blanket over them both, and his arms were wrapped securely around his torso.

The feeling of intimacy caused a warm burst to flutter in his gut . . . his prick, too.

At least I still feel arousal.

Oliver had been a little worried that he would be put off enjoying the touch of another.

Not Keith, though.

In fact, if Oliver wasn't mistaken, he could feel a thick rod pressing into his belly.

Oh, what I wouldn't give to be able to play with that . . . feel that moving in my ass.

Except, in all the times they'd played in the shower, Oliver had never taken the lead. He'd happily accepted Keith's ministrations, loving the feel of his big body surrounding his much leaner frame. Keith's hands on Oliver's body always felt absolutely amazing, but he'd never had the courage to push for more.

Would Keith allow me to explore?

Oliver wanted to find out. Unfortunately, when he went to move his arms so he could ease down Keith's body, they felt heavy and sluggish. Gritting his teeth, he tried harder. He felt beads of sweat pop out on his brow, but he managed to shift his weight and slide a few inches.

Keith's arms tightened around Oliver as he mumbled sleepily, "Stay, babe. It's too early."

With his lips twitching in amusement, Oliver peered up at Keith just in time to see the man's heavy-lidded eyes blink open. Keith smiled lazily at him.

"Mornin'," Keith mumbled. He squeezed Oliver's torso,

bringing his body back up his own. "Like this." Keith pressed his lips to Oliver's temple before nuzzling his lips over the sensitive flesh. "Not how it happened, but still love *this*."

Before Oliver could come up with a response, Keith slid a hand up to his jaw. He used the hold to turn Oliver's head, and he sealed his lips over Oliver's. With a nip and thrust of his tongue, Keith delved into Oliver's mouth — not asking, taking.

Oliver would have warned about morning breath — especially after all that had gone down — but from the way Keith lapped at his tongue, then suckled on it, he didn't seem to mind at all. Either that or he just didn't care. He plunged his tongue into Oliver's mouth, lapping along his teeth, mapping and teasing.

Keith ravished Oliver, holding him close and kissing him hungrily.

Going with it, Oliver sank into Keith's kiss. He quickly felt his body heat. His half-hard prick thickened swiftly to full hardness. Goose bumps broke out on his neck and upper arms, and his hips twitched with his need for pressure to his dick.

Oliver moaned into Keith's mouth and clutched at his shoulders. Digging in his fingers, he arched his back and rocked his hips, delighted to feel the hard length beneath him. The pressure sent a flash of delicious tingles through his groin, and he groaned again.

Unable to help himself, Oliver began rolling his hips in earnest, pressing against Keith's rod over and over.

Keith broke the kiss and groaned roughly. "Yessss, babe," he rumbled, lowering the arm around his waist to grip Oliver's ass. "You make me so fucking hot."

Feeling his balls draw up, Oliver grunted as he rested his forehead against Keith's collarbone. The way the bigger man rocked his hips to meet his ruts was the final straw. His testicles tightened, and his orgasm crashed over his senses.

Groaning with pleasure, Oliver unloaded in his jeans. Shudders worked through him as Keith massaged his ass cheek, extending his pleasure. Floating on the sweet bliss of release, Oliver heard Keith grunt just as he felt him buck beneath him . . . right before he moaned Oliver's name.

God, that sounds nice.

Panting harshly, Oliver floated happily on the endorphins from his release. He turned his face into Keith's neck and lapped lightly, enjoying the slight hint of sweat on his skin. With a sigh, he allowed himself to go completely lax, having faith that Keith wouldn't be expecting him to move.

"Wow, Oliver," Keith murmured after several moments of silence. "Hadn't meant to maul you first thing, but you're so hard to resist." He began rubbing his palms up and down Oliver's back. Keeping his voice soft, he asked, "How are you feeling today?"

Just that fast, Oliver's euphoria slipped away. He grimaced as he registered the cooling semen in his crotch. Shifting restlessly, he tipped his head a little, finding Keith staring down questioningly.

Oliver knew he needed to be honest. "A little weak still," he admitted. "And oddly tired."

Keith's brows furrowed as he nodded once. "You're recovering from a hell of a shock to your system." Concern morphed over his features. "Shit. I didn't take advantage of you, did I? I would never mean to do that. I — "

Easing his hand up, Oliver touched his forefingers to Keith's lips, ceasing his clearly concerned words. "You didn't take advantage of me," he assured. Still seeing Keith's worry in his light-brown eyes, Oliver told him, "I was trying to slither down your chest so I could check out what you're packing when you woke."

Relief filled Keith's face, removing the stress lines. Just as quickly, a sly smile curved his lips. "Really?" His expression heated. "You want to see what I'm packin'?"

Oliver nodded. Fighting his urge to nibble his bottom lip — *God, how lame. I'm a grown-ass man* — he shared, "I've never been a passive lover before. Not like I've been in the showers with you." They'd never talked about what they were doing, and Oliver struggled with how to voice his thoughts. "I've, well — " Taking the plunge, he told him, "There were so many times I wanted to turn around and drop to my knees. Or pull out a condom and ask you to fuck me." Oliver grimaced and added, "I wasn't sure if you were interested in more, and I wasn't certain that was an appropriate place to share. Then we never talked about it."

As Oliver had explained, the heat in Keith's eyes slowly banked. Although it didn't disappear completely, there was understanding in his gaze, too. Keith's lips curved into a small smile, and happiness shown on his features.

"I'm really happy to hear that, Oliver," Keith told him, rubbing circles with his fingers on the back of his neck that caused the hairs on his nape to stand on end. "I want more from you, too."

Oliver chuckled softly. "Guess we both need to work on our communication."

Keith grimaced as he shrugged one shoulder, his smile turning wry. "I always have, but you turned me down for a date. I was willing to accept what you'd give me. I didn't want to lose what small intimacy you were willing to share."

"Right," Oliver whispered.

Letting out a soft sigh, Oliver swallowed hard, knowing he had to share. He needed to explain what troubled him so much, regardless of how painful the memories remained, even after so much time. Oliver prayed he would be able to trust Keith.

"I haven't dated in a really long time because . . . because of Rodger." Oliver glanced at Keith. He saw the man's steady stare, the patience in his eyes, and he couldn't hold the handsome man's gaze. Focusing on the carefully manicured hairs of Keith's neck, Oliver continued. "He . . . he claimed to be bisexual, too, but that he wanted me. We dated. I thought we were exclusive."

Falling silent, Oliver swallowed again, trying to get more moisture into his too-dry throat.

After several seconds of quiet, Keith used his thumb to urge Oliver to tip his head a little. When their gazes met, Oliver saw the concern in Keith's brown eyes.

"You weren't exclusive, though, were you?" Keith guessed. When Oliver shook his head once, Keith offered, "You don't have to tell me if you don't want to."

"You should know," Oliver murmured. "Know the kind of baggage I carry."

Keith dipped his chin in a nod. "If that's what you wish, darling." He smiled warmly at him. "But I don't care what baggage you have as long as I get to keep doing things like this with you."

"I don't trust easily," Oliver admitted, knowing he couldn't take the man's out. "Rodger had already been dating some woman for six months before he started dating me." He felt his cheeks heat at the memory of being duped. "We'd been together for over five months, and I even had delusions of moving in together when I found out by accident."

Continuing to massage Oliver's neck, Keith stayed silent, waiting patiently while holding his gaze.

Appreciating the quiet support, Oliver managed to share, "I went out to eat with friends. There was a party going on in the private back room." He took a fortifying breath and revealed, "I recognized Rodger when he came out to use the men's room. I was about to stand and go say hello to him when another man heading back inside clapped him on the shoulder and said, *Congrats, man. You and Winona are a perfect couple. My bet is on your marriage lasting the distance, so don't let me down.*"

"Shit," Keith mumbled. "I'm sorry that happened to you."

Oliver scoffed as anger began to simmer within him. "He called me the next day. Had the audacity to ask if he could come see me." Frowning, Oliver stated, "That was when it hit me. We rarely ever went out, and when we did, it was to places out of the city, or we were placed discreetly in the back. I thought it was all about the romance, but now I know better. He was hiding."

"What did you say?"

It took Oliver a second to process Keith's question. Then he recalled he hadn't finished the story. "I asked him when he was getting married to Winona."

Keith's eyes widened, and he barked a surprised laugh. "Shit, babe. What did he say?"

With a sneer, Oliver answered, "He said he could explain, and it wasn't what I thought."

"Damn, really?" Frowning, Keith shook his head. "What an asshole."

"I told him I wasn't interested in any more of his lies and hung up on him. He called a few more times before eventually stopping." After a second, Oliver admitted, "That was almost six years ago."

After licking his lip, his expression turning serious, Keith murmured, "Are you still in love with him?"

Oliver's eyes widened in surprise. "No. No way." Realizing why the handsome man asked, he told him, "I just decided that fuck-buddies were easier. No chance of a broken heart."

Still serious, Keith quietly asked, "Will you give *me* a chance at being more than a fuck-buddy, Oliver?"

With his heart thudding in his chest, Oliver knew this was the moment of truth. Was he ready to head out on that limb again? Was he ready to give Keith that much power over him?

As Oliver stared into Keith's gorgeous brown eyes, he realized the man hid nothing from him. He saw patience, hope, and desire all rolled into one. Knowing how much the man wanted him, coupled with the fact that the sexy man had dropped everything the evening before to save him, and Oliver knew his answer.

"Yes." Oliver's pulse raced wildly through his veins at that admission, but he shoved his unease way down deep. "Yes, I want to try with you."

"Thank you." Keith leaned up and pecked an oh-so-light kiss to his lips. With intensity lighting his eyes, he added, "You won't regret it."

Oliver sure hoped not. Instead of commenting on that, he quipped, "Well, you've already proven your ability to save me, so . . ."

To Oliver's confusion, Keith's brows furrowed. "Is that why you're agreeing to this?" He cocked his head a little. "Because I stopped that man? I would have done it for a friend, too. That had nothing to do with my attraction to you."

"This isn't just some Florence Nightingale syndrome," Oliver assured, rubbing his fingertips along Keith's jaw, enjoying the slight scruff he felt there. "I was attracted to you from the beginning. Surely you know that."

Keith held his gaze for a long moment. Oliver did his best to keep his expression open. Finally, Keith seemed to find what he was looking for, and he nodded.

"So." Oliver shifted his legs and hips restlessly. "Do you think I can get a shower or something?" Feeling the dried cum tug at his pubes, he winced. "I could really stand to get out of these jeans."

Jeans were one of his least-favorite clothes to fall asleep in, but he understood why Keith hadn't undressed him. The man had probably figured he needed the armor to feel safe. He'd been right, and the blanket wrapped around him had added another layer of perceived protection.

The man is just way too perceptive.

"Definitely." Keith winced as he began shifting them. Then he chuckled. "I'm right there with you."

With a rueful laugh, Oliver fought against the heat rising in his cheeks, appreciating his dark skin.

After Keith had slipped out from under him, Oliver pushed carefully to a sitting position. When he tried to stand, his legs refused to hold his weight.

"No need to overdo it, Oliver," Keith rumbled, easing his arm around him and encouraging him to lean against him. "I got you."

Oliver nodded as he allowed Keith to help him out of the room. Spotting a clock on the wall, he winced. "Is that really the time?"

"It is," Keith confirmed. "But don't worry. Jimmy called in to your job site and let the foreman know you'd been in an accident." With a wink, he added, "And if they want a doctor's note, Ryan's partner will write you one."

Relief filled Oliver. Detective Ryan's partner was Doctor Morgan Pruitt. He didn't know how Keith had done it, but he seemed to have all the bases covered.

CHAPTER NINE

Keith knew Oliver was feeling overwhelmed, regardless of how well he hid it. His smiles were tight, and there were lines around his eyes. He looked around every corner of Keith's home as if someone would jump out at him.

Only time—and probably catching his attacker—would help Oliver settle.

And I can give him all the support he'll need.

Plus, Keith knew that their friends would be there by Oliver's side. After he'd helped Oliver into the shower, leaving him relaxing on his large shower bench with a new toothbrush and a tube of toothpaste, along with pointing out the standard supplies, he'd gone in search of clean sweats and a shirt that would fit him. Keith had found his phone and seen he had several messages.

It'd been a while since he'd slept through calls, but he appreciated that he had—and that they hadn't woken Oliver.

The first message had been from Richard—his college friend, who he'd started the firm with. "Hey, Keith. Is everything okay? Patrick told me you told him you had a family emergency and asked him to handle your morning meeting. When you get a chance, give me a call and let me know how we can help with your schedule."

Keith blew out a breath of relief, appreciating that Patrick had the initiative to make certain his work was covered. He would have to send the man a thank you card or something.

The second message was from Jimmy. "Hey, Keith. Thanks

76

again for last night. I'm listed as Oliver's next of kin for medical stuff, so Randy was okay to talk to me." There was a bit of a pause, then a soft sigh. "I know you said it wasn't my fault, and in my head, I understand, but I still feel damn guilty. Randy said it'd be best if Oliver was on fluids and broths for a couple of days. Will you let me know what you guys want? I really want to help. It'd make me feel better. Call me, please."

Shaking his head, even as Keith smiled, he shot a text to Jimmy. *Just got your message. I'll talk to Oliver and let you know. Call you soon.*

The third message was from Ryan, and Keith's smile disappeared. "This is Ryan. I have some information for Oliver. When he's up and ready to see me, call me."

Keith prayed it was good news . . . like the asshole had already been caught.

To Keith's surprise, he had a fourth message . . . from his mother. "This is Mother, Keith. I've received some disturbing information. Call me immediately."

Huh.

Frowning at his phone, Keith debated on whether or not to call her. The continued running of the shower drew his attention, so he decided against it. She could wait for a little while, at least. Oliver was more important.

Keith placed his phone on the dresser and began undressing. Hissing, he carefully peeled his slacks and underwear away from his groin. Then he shoved everything off, leaving it in a pile on the floor.

From his dresser, Keith pulled out two pairs of sweatpants, one long-sleeved sleep-shirt and one short-sleeved. Then he strode into his ensuite bathroom where he'd left Oliver. He saw the man right where he'd left him, although he was in the process of washing his braids.

The first time Keith had seen it, he'd found the process interesting. Oliver would gently massage the shampoo into his scalp, holding up his braids. He would use the natural downward flow of the water to pull the suds through the braids and out of his hair.

"You're sexy when you do that," Keith stated softly, hoping he didn't startle his new lover. One look at the gorgeous man had a predictable reaction to his prick, hardening quickly. The fact that Keith had had an orgasm less than an hour ago didn't seem to matter. When Oliver met his gaze, an amused tilt to his full lips, Keith added with a wink, "It helps that it means you have your arms up, putting your lean sexy torso and gorgeous erection on clear display."

Oliver snorted.

As he continued to do that, Keith took a quick slip under the water to wet his own short hair. He washed swiftly, then conditioned. Just as he was finishing rinsing that, he felt hands on his shaft.

Groaning, Keith looked down and appreciated the sight — and feel — before him. Oliver had leaned forward on the seat. He had one hand on Keith's hard prick, jacking slowly. With his other palm, he cradled Keith's balls.

Keith sighed deeply, enjoying his lover's ministrations. The tug on his rod, the feel of his palm sliding over his firm flesh, and the wonderfully gentle massage to his balls were creating a myriad of exquisite tingles. Oliver's hands were the stuff of legends.

"God, Oliver," Keith crooned, beginning to rock into the man's hold. "The things you do to me." When Oliver skimmed the nail of his forefinger behind his balls, stimulating his prostate from the outside, Keith groaned and spread his legs wider. "Yessss," he hissed, expressing his enjoyment.

Oliver didn't disappoint. He reached farther, deeper, and teased over Keith's hole.

"Oliver," Keith cried, bucking in Oliver's hold. The base of his spine tingled, his release threatening. "C-Close."

With a cheeky smile, Oliver opened his mouth, leaned forward, and swallowed his cock to the root.

Shouting Oliver's name, Keith came. His knees trembled as his orgasm rolled through him, threatening to buckle. He grabbed the top of the shower stall as well as the washcloth rack as a hard shudder rocked through him.

Staring in slack-jawed shock, Keith watched Oliver drink his release, all the while staring right up at him. The erotic sight caused his balls to force out an extra spurt. Black spots flashed across Keith's vision, and he groaned his lover's name.

Finally, the suction became too much, and Keith would forever deny the whine that escaped him.

Oliver immediately pulled off, allowing his half-mast dick to slip from between his lips. Panting hard, Keith watched Oliver lick his lips obscenely. His dark eyes gleamed in the bathroom light as he smiled at him.

"You taste fantastic," Oliver murmured as he grabbed the soap. "Yum."

Groaning, Keith muttered, "Your mouth is killer."

With a chuckle, Oliver began washing him. He started at Keith's groin before moving on to his abdominals and nipples. His movements were slow, betraying his continued fatigue, but upon seeing the gleam of determination lighting his dark eyes, Keith didn't question him. His lover wanted this so Keith would give it to him.

When Oliver indicated, Keith bent, so his lover could wash his arms, pits, and neck. Then Oliver turned his attention to Keith's legs. Doing as Oliver bid, Keith lifted each foot onto the seat, one at a time.

Keith couldn't remember anyone ever taking such good care of him.

"Oliver," Keith muttered when Oliver reached between his legs to wash his crack and ass.

With one soapy finger, Oliver pressed lightly against his muscle. "Are you a switch, Keith?"

Swallowing hard, Keith admitted, "I don't know."

Petting Keith's opening gently without pushing, Oliver cocked his head. "Don't know? Never been fucked, or never fucked at all?"

Keith licked his lips, then admitted, "Never been fucked." He held Oliver's gaze as he told him, "Until you, no one has ever even tried to touch me there . . . but I like it."

Oliver smiled widely. "I think I like that." Easing his hands back to Keith's thighs, he urged him to put his foot down. "I'm mostly a bottom, but eventually, I know I'll want to plow your ass."

Nodding, Keith stated, "I think I'd like that, too."

Keith felt his stomach flutter upon seeing Oliver's smile widen even further.

"Okay." Oliver straightened, revealing his hard-on. He wrapped his hand around his black length and began to slowly stroke. Peering at Keith through his lashes, Oliver asked, "Think you can help me with this?"

Groaning, Keith instantly dropped to his knees. He batted his lover's hand away from the gorgeous piece of male flesh. Easing Oliver's legs wide, Keith bent over his man's groin and swallowed around his crown.

Keith relished the loud moan. When he teased over Oliver's ball sack, the man murmured Keith's name appreciatively and spread his legs wider. Recalling Oliver's words, he grabbed the conditioner as he bobbed on the man's length. Keith wasn't very experienced at giving a blowjob, and he couldn't take his lover all the way, but he knew other ways to give pleasure.

After Keith poured a healthy dollop of conditioner onto the fingers of his left hand, he tossed aside the bottle. Then he gripped the base of Oliver's erection with that hand. Keith pressed one slippery finger between his lover's cheeks, finding his opening. Without hesitation, Keith slid his middle finger deep into the man.

Sucking strongly as he pulled partway off, Keith crooked his finger, searching. He found it swiftly, Oliver's prostate, causing the man to cry out with bliss. Setting up a smooth rhythm, Keith worked his lover's chute and shaft.

Oliver's trembles, whines, and shudders caused a fresh wash of arousal to warm his groin. Smiling around his mouthful of cock, he knew he couldn't get up again — not right away, anyway. Still, his prick was giving it the good ol' college try.

A moment later, Oliver grabbed Keith's head and jolted. He bucked, shoving his prick deep into his mouth. Only Keith's hand wrapped around the base of Oliver's cock kept him from gagging as the first burst of cum flooded Keith's mouth.

Keith recovered quickly, moving his hand from Oliver's dick to his hip, holding him still. Easing his head up a little as he swallowed, he caught the next shot of cream on his tongue, allowing him to taste his lover's seed. The slightly salty goodness lit up his taste buds, and Keith moaned appreciatively.

Oliver rewarded him with one, two more spurts, and Keith happily saved his lover's flavor. In the past, he'd always used condoms. Oliver's flesh tasted so much better than latex.

Easing off Oliver's softening prick, Keith straightened on his knees. He gripped his man's nape with his clean hand, leaned forward, and sealed his lips over the other man's. Kissing had been reserved for women in the past, but not with Oliver. With Oliver, Keith wanted everything.

As Keith delved deep into Oliver's mouth, he tasted his own cum's flavor on his tongue, mixed with mint from the toothpaste he'd left him with when he'd gone to get clothes. Underneath that was a fresh masculine flavor all Oliver's own.

After breaking the kiss, Keith put a few inches between their faces. He grinned at the man. "You know, not that I minded your morning breath, but you taste much better now."

Oliver barked a laugh, grinning at him. "You, too."

Keith grunted before taking Oliver's mouth again. A shiver worked down his spine, and he realized the water was getting cold. Feeding Oliver a chuckle, he continued to kiss him for another moment before breaking away.

"We better get out before we freeze," Keith told Oliver as he rose to his feet. He shut off the water, then stepped from the stall. "Let me get you a towel." After grabbing one off the warming rack, Keith turned back to Oliver, who hadn't moved, looking relaxed, sated, and sexy on his shower's tile seat. "God, you are so fucking sexy."

Oliver chuckled, smiling up at him. "Thanks."

Seeing the goose bumps breaking out on Oliver's skin, Keith quickly pulled his head out of his ass. He held out his hand. After Oliver took it, he helped his recovering lover to his feet.

Keith swiftly rubbed the towel over Oliver, drying him. Once finished, he helped him into the sweatpants. He needed to roll up the cuffs a couple of times, but the drawstring waist allowed them to be kept up. Keith followed that up with the long-sleeved shirt before leading him to his bedroom.

After having Oliver sit on the bed, Keith told him, "Just give me a minute to dry and dress. Then we'll go to the bar in the kitchen for breakfast."

In response, Oliver's stomach growled, and both men laughed.

Hurrying through his own dry and dress, Keith mentally prepared himself for the conversation he would need to have with Oliver. He also tried to recall what kind of soup he might have in his cupboards. While soup wasn't a normal breakfast choice, Keith needed to follow Randy's guidance.

"Okay," Keith began, returning to Oliver. "Ready for breakfast?"

Oliver's stomach rumbled again.

Keith grinned, holding out his arm. "Then let's go."

That time, when Oliver stood, his legs seemed to hold him. His movements were slow, and he gripped Keith's arm for balance, but he didn't need to lean on him. Together, they made their way back to the kitchen.

Leaving Oliver sitting on a padded barstool, Keith rounded the bar and went to the cupboard. He pulled out two coffee mugs and set them on the counter. When he picked up the carafe, which had automatically processed due to the timer, he paused.

"Uh, guess we didn't ask Randy if you could have coffee," Keith mused, worry filling him. Seeing the pleading in Oliver's eyes as he stuck out his bottom lip in a puppy-dog look, Keith laughed. "Okay. One cup, and drink it slow . . . just in case."

Keith filled both mugs before returning the carafe to the warming plate. As he carried both to the counter, he asked, "Creamer, milk, sugar?" He smirked. "Something else?"

"A dash of milk or creamer. Whatever you have is fine. I'm not picky," Oliver told him. As Keith headed toward the refrigerator, he cocked his head and asked, "Uh, what's something else?"

Snorting, Keith pulled both a pumpkin spice creamer as well as a jug of two-percent milk from his refrigerator. As he placed them on the bar, he admitted, "Believe it or not, I knew a guy in college who used to put honey in his coffee."

Oliver made a face of disgust. "Honey?"

Keith nodded. "Yep."

"Ugh." Oliver picked up the creamer. "That's terrible."

"Eh. Honestly, it wasn't that bad," Keith admitted. Seeing

Oliver's eyes widen in shock, he told him, "I tried it once. Not something I'd want every day, but it was drinkable."

"Yeah, okay," Oliver replied, drawing out his words while pinning him with a narrow-eyed stare. He shook his head once before turning his attention to his coffee.

Dropping the subject, Keith picked up his own mug and took a sip. He hummed, enjoying the rich flavor of his high-end coffee. Richard had laughed and called him a coffee snob on more than one occasion when Keith had insisted on a certain brand of bean be purchased for the office due to the expense.

Who cares? Totally worth it.

Keith enjoyed a few more sips before placing the mug back on the bar. "So, I think I have chicken noodle soup and clam chowder," he told Oliver, moving toward his pantry. "I know that's not normal breakfast fair, but Randy said soup or broth to start." Opening his pantry, Keith heard Oliver sigh, clearly unhappy with his choices. Spotting something else on the shelf, Keith offered, "Oh. I also have one of those instant *Ramen* lunch soup cups." Picking it up, he showed it to Oliver. "It's chicken flavored with bits of carrots and corn."

To Keith's pleasure, Oliver's expression brightened.

"That'll work," Oliver told him, cradling his coffee mug. "Thanks."

"You're welcome," Keith replied automatically as he began removing the wrapper off the package.

"If you don't mind me saying, you don't seem like a *Ramen* kind of guy." Oliver pointed at Keith as he added, "You're just so fit."

Keith laughed, feeling his cheeks heat. "Well, this shit may be my guilty pleasure."

"*May* be?" Oliver teased.

Nodding, while adding water to the *Styrofoam* cup, Keith shared with his lover, "I don't have a sweet tooth. I'm more into salty." As he placed the container in the microwave and started it, he told him, "Yeah. Give me peanuts or popcorn over chocolate any day."

"Huh."

Upon hearing Oliver's non-committal noise, Keith turned to face him. He crossed his arms over his chest, arching one brow in silent question.

Oliver grinned. "Then we make a good pair. I'll take the chocolate and leave the peanuts to you."

Keith returned Oliver's grin. "Sounds good to me."

Chapter Ten

Oliver watched Keith pause the episode of *Survivor* they were watching. Relaxing on the sofa, he tracked his lover as the big man crossed to the foyer. For a few seconds, he felt his heart rate increase when Keith disappeared from sight.

After a couple of slow deep breaths, Oliver managed to get his racing pulse under control. He knew it was a side effect of being attacked, but that didn't make the response any easier to control. Oliver knew it was irrational, that the boogey man wasn't around every corner, but some things just weren't rational—fear being one of them.

When Oliver heard Keith greet someone, then Jimmy's voice as he responded softly, he let out a long sigh.

I'll get through this.

Oliver refused to think otherwise. Besides, he had plenty of friends to help. As Keith led the way into the room, Oliver smiled.

A sexy boyfriend, too.

For the first time in six years, the idea of having a boyfriend again didn't cause a shaft of fear, of a desire to run, to course through him.

"Ollie," Jimmy cried, rushing toward him.

"Hey, Jimmy." Oliver held out his hand. "Thanks for coming."

"Of course!" Jimmy placed the bags he'd been carrying on the floor, then jumped onto the sofa beside him. He wrapped his arms around Oliver's torso and cuddled close, even resting his head on his shoulder. "How are you?"

Oliver sighed as he wrapped his left arm around Jimmy's waist. Resting his temple across the top of Jimmy's head, he relaxed in the familiar hold. He and Jimmy had been there for each other since third grade.

"I'm a little jumpy," Oliver admitted. He never lied to his bestie. Feeling Keith sit down on his other side, Oliver rested his hand on the man's thigh, relieved when he instantly took it and threaded their fingers. "Keith is making it better."

Jimmy tipped his head a little, obviously looking down. Then his head popped up so fast that Oliver almost didn't move his own in time. His bestie stared at him with wide blue eyes.

Oliver smiled.

"Oh my god!" Jimmy cried, a wide grin spreading across his face. "You did it. You finally admit that you're dating." In the next instant, Jimmy glared at Keith. "You better treat Oliver right, or I'm gonna have Vance and Brand on your ass."

To Oliver's relief, Keith chuckled, obviously not upset. He even replied, "After all the time I spent wooing Oliver, getting him to give me a chance?" He shook his head. "Not happening." Then Keith brought their twined fingers to his lips and pressed a kiss to Oliver's knuckles.

Jimmy beamed, giving away his pleasure at that response. His gaze strayed to the TV, and his jaw sagged open. He snapped his attention to Keith.

"You're watching *Survivor* with Oliver?" Jimmy's eyes rounded as his voice grew hushed. "Wow. You really *are* perfect for him."

Oliver felt his cheeks heat, silently appreciating his dark skin.

At the same time, Keith told him, "It's interesting. It's a fascinating study in the rise, fluidity, and decline of a human society."

Arching one brow, Oliver asked, "Human society?"

"Sure," Keith replied with a nod. "The groups form their own little tribe, and a tribe hierarchy and division of tasks quickly arises. They learn from each other, so they can switch things up, creating fluidity." He continued to explain, "Then the challenges and tribal council creates dissension and distrust, causing the decline of the tribe." Keith shrugged. "It's fascinating. Plus, the obstacle challenges are fun to watch."

Jimmy barked a laugh.

Oliver nodded. "Huh," he mused. "Never thought about it like that before."

Keith leaned over and pecked a kiss to Oliver's lips. "Just my take on it." Then he straightened and pointed at Jimmy's bags. "What'd you bring?"

Bouncing off the sofa, Jimmy grabbed the bags and placed them on the cushion instead. "I went to your place and packed two bags of clothes," he told them, pointing at first one, then a second. "This third one is food. Some of your favorite comfort foods as well as stuff that Randy said to have."

"Rocky Road?" Oliver immediately asked.

"Of course," Jimmy replied with a roll of his eyes. "As if I'd forget." He turned to Keith while batting away Oliver's reaching hand. "Where's your kitchen? I'll put it away."

Keith used his thumb to point over his shoulder before rising from the sofa. "Why don't you take Oliver to the study over there? I'm sure he's ready to get dressed in some of his own clothes." He pointed across the foyer and at a pair of closed French doors. "I'll put the food away."

Oliver hesitated an instant, then nodded. "Okay." It would be nice to put on his own stuff, making him feel more normal. On the other hand, Oliver rather enjoyed wearing his lover's stuff. Unable to help himself, he blurted, "You don't like me wearing your stuff?"

Pinning him with a scorching look that left no room for misunderstanding, Keith told him, "Oh, Oliver. I *love* seeing you in my clothes." He growled softly as he swept his gaze down his body, then back up to meet his eyes. "There's something very primal about it. I just thought *you* would be more comfortable."

Scoffing softly, Oliver couldn't help the slight huskiness in his voice as he answered, "Maybe when we're not expecting more company."

Just that fast, Keith's expression sobered. "Sounds like a plan." Then he bent, pecked a kiss to Oliver's cheek, and headed out of the room.

Jimmy fanned himself. "Damn."

Oliver smiled at his friend. "I know, right?" Blowing out a breath, he shook his head. "Not sure what he sees in me, but I sure love how he makes me feel."

Blowing a raspberry, Jimmy rested his hands on his hips. "The only reason I'm not smacking you upside the back of your head is because you're recovering," he declared, scowling at him. "You're awesome, and you deserve to be treated awesome." Then Jimmy held out his hand and ordered, "Come on. You'll love the choices I brought."

Oliver took Jimmy's hand and allowed himself to be tugged to his feet. To his relief, he felt pretty steady when his friend released him. While Oliver still moved slowly, at least he was moving well again.

"Thank you for taking care of my work for me," Oliver stated, following Jimmy, who'd scooped up the two bags and started toward where Keith had indicated.

Jimmy smiled over his shoulder at him. "Of course. That's what brothers from another mother do."

Chuckling softly, Oliver followed Jimmy into the study.

Thirty minutes later, dressed in his own clothes and feeling more like himself, Oliver sat back on the sofa. Once again, the show was paused, and Keith headed toward the front door.

That time, however, Jimmy remained to his left on the sofa.

Oliver clutched Jimmy's hand like a lifeline. He heard Keith open the door and greet someone. The deep tones of Detective Ryan Straton responded, and Oliver gulped loudly.

"It'll be okay," Jimmy whispered into his ear. "Ryan will get this guy. He and Carl are great detectives."

Nodding, Oliver knew he needed to believe that with his whole heart. He wouldn't be able to truly relax otherwise.

Staring at the archway, Oliver spotted Keith first. His lover hurried back to him as both Ryan and Carl appeared behind him. Once Keith sat, he immediately took Oliver's other hand.

"It's good to see you feeling better, Oliver." Ryan smiled at him. Even as the detective glanced between everyone's joined hands, he didn't miss a beat. "We have some information for you, and for the most part, I think it's good."

"Okay," Oliver murmured.

Keith waved toward a couple of chairs off to the right. "Please, have a seat." Then he sighed and shook his head. "Sorry about the bad manners. Can I get you guys anything to drink? Coffee or something?"

"Water would be nice," Carl replied for them both before focusing on Oliver. "And I'm very sorry for what happened to you, Oliver, but Clayton delaying that guy and Keith stepping in may have blown this case wide open."

"I'll get the water," Jimmy claimed, jumping to his feet before Keith could move. "Be right back."

"I'll take some, too, please," Oliver murmured.

Jimmy nodded and smiled. "Waters all around."

Keith gave him a grateful-looking nod. "What did you find?" he asked.

"First." Ryan rose to his feet and opened a file Oliver hadn't even noticed he'd been carrying. "Do you recognize this person?" He pulled an eight-by-twelve photo from his folder and placed it on the coffee table before them.

Oliver gasped, a chill racing down his spine. While his vision had been a little fuzzy, the blond man in the photo looked disturbingly like his attacker. He wished he could see the man's teeth to be certain.

"I-I'm pretty sure that's him," Oliver told Ryan. Meeting his gaze, he added, "My vision was a little fuzzy, and what I really remember is that he was missing a front tooth."

Ryan exchanged a look with Carl, then pulled a second photo from his file. That picture was a sketch of a man's face. The hair was a little longer, but the features were extremely similar. In the sketch, the guy sported a creepy smile that Oliver recognized all too well, and the man was indeed missing a front tooth.

Suddenly, Oliver found breathing difficult. He would forever deny the whimper that escaped his throat. Spots flashed across his vision as a shudder worked through his body.

In the next instant, Oliver felt a hand on his nape. He was pushed forward until his head was between his knees. Another hand rubbed up and down his back, clearly trying to soothe him.

"Easy, babe," Keith crooned into his ear. "Focus on slow, even breaths. You can do it. You're in my home. You're safe."

Oliver gripped Keith's hand tightly, so he wasn't certain who else was touching him. Still, focusing on not only his lover's words, but also his touch, Oliver did his best to obey. He stared at the light-blue area rug beneath the sofa.

After who knew how long, Oliver's pulse began to slow. His breathing eased. He even managed to ease his death-grip on Keith's fingers.

"S-Sorry," Oliver muttered, feeling a wash of embarrassment.

Good grief.

"Nothing to be sorry for," Keith murmured into his ear. "Your psyche is working through a trauma. We'll get through this."

Then Oliver felt Keith kiss his temple.

Oliver nodded, took one more fortifying breath, then began to straighten. The hands on his back and neck immediately disappeared. In the next instant, a glass of water appeared before him.

Okay. Bet at least one of the hands was Jimmy's.

"Thanks, Jimmy," Oliver whispered, taking the glass. He sipped it once, twice, before braving a slightly larger mouthful. Finally, Oliver swept his focus around the room. Blowing out a breath, he offered the detectives a wan smile. "Um, guess that means I recognize him."

Both Ryan and Carl were on their feet before their chairs, watching intently. They exchanged another glance before settling back in their seats.

Ryan rubbed a palm over his bearded cheeks before saying, "Keith remembering the license plate number of the guy trying to take you led us to this guy. Dale Kavins." He pointed at what must have been a DMV photo. "When we ran his information, it pinged an open case." Ryan pointed at the sketch. "Well, three open cases. All the victims agreed that this sketch was the guy who did it."

After swallowing hard, Oliver asked, "Did what?"

"Drugging, kidnapping, and raping his victims," Carl answered, his voice soft.

"Th-Three others," Oliver whispered before taking another sip of his water to alleviate his suddenly dry throat.

"That's just the ones who've come forward." Ryan grimaced, shaking his head. "Some refuse to go to the cops. They just want to forget the whole thing happened."

Guilt flooded Oliver. If he'd had his way, he would have been one of those people. He didn't want to think about it, either.

"Hey, I know what you're thinking," Keith rumbled, lifting his hand to his lips and kissing his palm. "We all know you would have let Carl and Ryan know eventually."

Oliver shook his head as he met Keith's gaze. "I don't know about that, Keith," he admitted sadly. "I think I would have just hid what happened because I didn't want to deal with it."

While Oliver knew it made him look bad, it was the truth.

"With the support of your friends, you would have dealt with it properly," Jimmy countered, rubbing his back. "Just like we're dealing with it now. Together."

Forcing a smile, Oliver decided not to counter his bestie.

"Where do we go from here?" Keith asked, frowning at the pictures. "What's next?"

"Is this Dale guy in jail, yet?" Jimmy asked what Oliver really wanted to know.

"Not yet," Ryan told him. "Detective Lance Brody is the one who caught the original case." Grimacing, he added, "So we had to explain about you and why we were looking into the guy. He went over there with back-up to pick him up, but Dale wasn't there." Holding Jimmy's gaze, Ryan assured, "We'll get him. We're monitoring his home and his place of work. We've subpoenaed his financials, so we can figure out where his haunts are. We're digging into his life for friends and family." Ryan's deep brown eyes narrowed as he vowed, "We *will* get this dirtbag."

Oliver nodded as he blew out a soft breath. "Okay." Then he grimaced. "Wow, the fourth guy."

"Uh, actually, the second guy," Carl corrected. "This douche bag is an equal opportunity rapist." Shaking his head, he stated, "Guess he spots someone he wants, male or female, and decides instead of asking, he just takes."

"It's a power play," Oliver whispered, recalling the prior evening. "He said . . . said he knew I could hear him. Said that knocking me out completely wouldn't be as much fun. He likes his victims to be aware of what's happening to them." Fighting a shiver, Oliver added, "And he takes pictures. He likes to write our names on our pictures."

"Shit," Ryan muttered, peering at Carl. "He takes trophies."

"And we know what kind of person takes trophies," Carl muttered, shaking his head.

"A serial." Ryan nodded. "Except this time, he's not a serial murderer. He's a serial rapist."

"Who won't stop until he's forced to stop," Carl added. After a nod from Ryan, he turned his attention back to Oliver. "I know this is hard and completely sucks, but will you please walk us through everything you remember about last night?"

Oliver took in a slow, deep breath before letting it out again. He knew it needed to be done, but that didn't mean he had to like it. After receiving an encouraging squeeze from Keith's hand and feeling Jimmy curl against his side in support, Oliver gave his statement, walking through everything he could remember.

CHAPTER ELEVEN

After everyone had left, Keith wanted to do nothing but bundle Oliver into his arms, carry him up the stairs into his room, and hide away from the world for the rest of the day.

Too bad life didn't work that way.

They hadn't been alone fifteen minutes when Keith's phone rang. Looking at the screen, he groaned.

"Is everything okay?" Oliver asked.

Keith smiled at Oliver and held up his ringing phone. "It's my mother." Allowing his smile to turn wry, he added, "I'm considering ignoring it, but—"

"I understand," Oliver assured. He shrugged. "Family. What can you do?"

Nodding, Keith answered the call. "Hello, Mother," he greeted. "How are you today?"

"Hello, son," Diana Ryzor responded in a clipped tone. "And don't act all innocent with me. I left you a message hours ago. Why haven't you called me back?"

"I'm sorry, Mother." Keith did his best to keep his voice even. If his mother thought he was upset with her, the call would take twice as long. "I've been busy."

"You can't be all *that* busy," his mother countered. "I tried the office after leaving you a message. Candice said you weren't at the office today. Come over immediately."

Keith watched Oliver rise from the sofa and head toward the kitchen. His gaze fell on his lover's ass in his form-fitting, faded blue jeans. The only reason Keith didn't hum with approval was because he heard his mother snap his name.

"Keith Ryzor. Are you paying attention to me?"

Pinching the bridge of his nose, Keith replied, "I'm sorry, Mother. I did say I was busy with something. I'm not going to be able to come to you right now."

Oliver paused in the doorway and turned to face him. "If you need to go, it's okay," he told him, although his smile appeared a little tremulous.

Keith narrowed his eyes and shook his head. "I don't want you alone right now."

"It's only been a few minutes. I can text Jimmy and have him turn around," Oliver countered. "He'll do it in a heartbeat. You know that."

"Who are you talking to?" Diana demanded. "What is this so-called important business that makes you unavailable?"

Shit!

He'd forgotten to lower his phone from his mouth. Instead of answering his mother's question, he told her, "Just a minute." That time, he remembered to place the phone against his jeans to muffle the speaker when he asked Oliver, "Are you certain?"

Nodding, Oliver admitted, "If my mother called and needed to see me, even after all this time, I'd still drop everything and go."

Keith didn't want to point out the very big differences in their situations, so he just nodded. "Okay. Confirm that Jimmy can come back first."

Oliver nodded and whipped out a quick text.

Bringing his phone back to his ear, Keith was just in time to hear his mother snap, "Keith Jacob Ryzor, why are you ignoring me? That is no way to treat your mother. You—"

"I'm sorry, Mother," Keith cut in, something he rarely did to the woman who gave birth to him. Except, he knew telling her that he had a boyfriend wasn't something he should do over the phone. "I need to be certain it's okay to leave before confirming I can come see you. Please be patient."

"Leave?" Diana instantly turned suspicious. "Leave where? What's going on? Is it a legal matter? Are the cops involved?"

Keith jumped on that out. "Yes, it's a legal matter, and the cops are involved." Before she could ask more questions that he wasn't ready to answer, he told her, "You know I can't discuss cases. Please, just give me a minute."

"Very well," his mother replied with a barely-there note in her voice that told him she was feeling put out. "I'll hold."

Swell.

Lowering his phone back to his leg, Keith heard Oliver's phone chime. His lover glanced at it, then smiled at Keith. He nodded.

"Jimmy's turning around. He'll be back here in ten."

Nodding, Keith returned to his call. "Are you at the estate or the vineyard?" he asked, referring to the private estate at the back of the vineyard as opposed to the business proper.

"The estate."

Damn.

"Okay. I'll see be there in less than thirty minutes," Keith told her.

"See that you are," his mother replied primly. "Good-bye." Then the line disconnected.

Ever the polite one, even when ordering people around.

Shaking his head, Keith crossed to Oliver, who'd been taking the water glasses to the kitchen. He slipped up behind the man where he stood at the sink, pouring out the glasses, and wrapped his arms around his waist. For just an instant, Oliver tensed. Then, to Keith's pleasure, the man relaxed back in his hold, offering him some of his weight.

Keith pressed a kiss to the side of Oliver's neck before nuzzling his cheek against it. "I'm sorry, babe," he rumbled softly. "I'll try not to be too long."

Oliver tipped his head to the side and peered over his shoulder at him. "Don't worry about it. Jimmy doesn't work today, so he can stay however long we need." His smile faded a bit before he said, "Maybe we should go to my place. Do you really want me in your space while you're not here?"

"Of course I do," Keith immediately replied. Hell, if he had his way, he would never allow the man to leave. After doing it once, Keith wanted to hold Oliver in his arms every night. Of course, he didn't say that to the man, knowing it was a sure-fire way to scare him off. Nuzzling his neck some more, Keith urged, "Relax. Watch TV. Raid the fridge. Enjoy yourselves. I'll be back before you know it."

To Keith's relief, Oliver nodded before turning his head and pressing a kiss to the underside of his chin. Goose bumps broke out on his skin, and Keith hummed. Pleasure flooded him as he realized that was the first time the man had initiated a kiss between them.

Just as Keith thought about turning Oliver around so he could kiss the man properly, his doorbell rang. He cut a look toward the clock on the microwave, thinking there had to be no way it'd been ten minutes.

Damn. Eight minutes. Jimmy must have hurried or hit all green lights.

Sighing, Keith eased backward. He pecked one more kiss to Oliver's neck. Then he headed toward the front of the house. As he strode toward the door, he realized he'd had more guests in the last twenty-four hours than he had in the last three months.

Huh. Go figure. I'm finally getting a life.

Unable to help himself, Keith grinned.

Even with all the upheaval he bet adding Oliver to his life would cause, he knew the man would be completely worth it.

Hmmm . . . upheaval.

Keith knew how to head that off . . . he hoped.

Opening the door, Keith greeted Jimmy. "Thanks for coming back, Jimmy." He shrugged as he admitted, "My mother is demanding my presence for some reason, and I don't want to leave Oliver alone."

"Are you going to tell your mother about Oliver?" Jimmy asked, clearly being nosey to protect his friend. "He doesn't deserve to be a dirty little secret."

"I would never do that to Oliver," Keith declared as he shut the door behind them. "And yes, I do plan to tell my family."

Keith knew at least one of them would be happy for him. "Oliver is washing the water cups in the kitchen," he revealed, leading the way. Lowering his voice, Keith added, "I think he just needs something to do."

Jimmy nodded. "He's normally a really active guy. I bet being so sedentary is driving him nuts."

"I don't blame him," Keith stated. "I'd feel the same way."

"Same way about what?" Oliver asked, peering over his shoulder at them as they walked into the kitchen.

Keith winked. "That I'm going to paddle your ass if you two start watching season three without me."

Oliver gaped while Jimmy barked a laugh.

Snorting, Keith shook his head. "Actually, that I'd be washing water glasses from boredom, too, if I were forced to recuperate for a few days."

Rolling his eyes as he chuckled, Oliver nodded. "Busted." He pulled his hands out of the water and dried them on a towel. "Just . . . normally I'm so busy. Ya know?" His dark brows furrowed, his eyebrow piercing glinting in the light, as he added, "But right now, I can't do shit for more than a few minutes before I get tired. It sucks."

"I totally understand," Keith told him, wrapping him in his arms, ignoring the dampness still on Oliver's hands when they landed on his polo-shirt-clad chest. He narrowed his eyes. "But I am serious about *Survivor*. No season three without me."

Smirking, Oliver quipped, "Maybe we'll watch season two, since you finished *that* without *me*."

Groaning, Keith tipped his head back. "I'm sorry, babe," he entreated. "I thought you were still awake."

Oliver chuckled. "I know."

"Okay. Be back as soon as I can." Keith pecked a kiss to Oliver's lips before pulling away. "See you shortly."

With a wave and good-bye to both men, Keith hurried to the front of his home. He slipped on a nice pair of shoes as well as his overcoat. Then Keith grabbed his phone and keys and headed to the garage.

Once Keith was on his way, he made a call to his sister.

"Hey, big bad lawyer bro," Trudy greeted perkily. "Why on earth are you calling me before noon? Need a rec on a great bottle of wine?"

Keith chuckled, loving hearing his sister's happy voice. "I always appreciate great recs on wine," he told her. Then he sobered. "But that's not the issue. Any idea what Mother's on about today?"

"No, what's up?" Trudy sounded just as confused as Keith felt.

Shaking his head, even knowing Trudy couldn't see him, Keith told her, "She's demanding I come see her. Says she discovered some disturbing information."

Huh. Could she already know I'm seeing a man?

If that was the case, back-up was even more important.

"Well, you know her," Trudy cajoled. "Finding out her party's china pattern duplicates someone else's is cause for emergency." Scoffing, his sister added, "I'm sure it can't be that serious."

"Party?" Confusion filled him.

Snickering, Trudy teased, "Did you forget about our annual fashionably late New Year's party? It happens the last

Saturday of January every year."

"Oh, that." Keith shook his head. "I remember." In fact, it would be a great time to introduce Oliver to his family. "While I'm talking to Mother, I'll have to remember to tell her that I need to add a plus-one to my reservation."

"Really?" Trudy squealed. "You're bringing a date?"

Keith grinned, knowing that would get his sister's attention. "I'm on my way to the estate now. Can you get away to hear all about it?"

Trudy snorted in a very unladylike fashion—a noise she would never allow their mother to hear her make. "Even if I wasn't, I'd beg off. What's your ETA?"

"Hmmm." Keith glanced at his dash's clock. "Seven minutes."

"Say no more. I'm on my way." Trudy sounded so very excited. "See you shortly."

Considering Keith hadn't seen Trudy in a good two weeks, he wasn't lying when he replied, "Can't wait." Then he disconnected and focused on driving.

In under ten minutes, Keith turned his *BMW* into the driveway of his parent's ancestral estate. His great, great grandfather had built the place using the proceeds of the vineyard after it had taken off. The sprawling, over five-thousand-foot home was designed in the style of a Mexican hacienda, complete with the white stucco walls, red-tiled roof, and rustic wood accents.

Keith spotted Trudy in a golf cart loitering at the edge of a narrow, paved path that led to the vineyard. As soon as he exited his vehicle, she hopped off the cart and skipped her way toward him. Her arms were outstretched, and her blonde hair was slipping from her messy bun due to her antics, stray wisps falling around her face.

Wrapping his arms around her, Keith caught his sister in a

tight hug. He grinned as he lifted her in the air and swung her in a circle. Then he placed her on her feet and pecked a kiss to her cheek.

Looping her arm through Keith's, Trudy grinned up at him. "So, who is this mystery woman that I know nothing about?" Her eyes widened just as quickly. "Oh, my god. Is she from the wrong side of the tracks, and that's why Mother is up in arms? Did you tell her about her before me?" As if that was exactly it, Trudy smacked Keith's chest as if punishing him.

Scoffing, Keith smirked at her. "No, and I'll tell you all about my special someone after dealing with Mother." Urging Trudy toward the house, he said, "Come on, sis."

Trudy hummed, as if she didn't believe him, but she accompanied him readily enough.

Keith entered the home he'd grown up in, spotting Jensen coming toward him across the central foyer. "Morning, Jensen," he greeted. He'd never heard the stiff and formal butler's first name, even after all these years. "How are you today?"

"I'm fine, sir," Jensen replied. He indicated the hallway to the left. "Your mother is awaiting you in the sunroom, sir."

"Thank you," Keith responded dutifully. "Will you have coffee and a light repast delivered to us, please?"

Jensen dipped his head in a regal nod. "It will be done, sir."

Keith thanked Jensen again, then began escorting Trudy in that direction. Noticing the way she started nibbling her lower lip, he murmured, "Stop worrying. You said yourself it's probably nothing."

Sighing, Trudy admitted, "That was before she had Jensen waiting for you."

Smirking to hide his own concern, Keith winked at Trudy. "Don't you remember," he teased. "Jensen is everywhere."

Trudy snickered.

They reached the sunroom, and Keith opened the door for Trudy. After his sister had entered, he followed her inside and closed the door behind them. Keith peered around the glass-enclosed space, easily spotting his mother in a gliding rocker to the left.

Following Trudy, Keith headed in that direction.

"Good morning, Mother," Keith greeted after Trudy had bent to give their mother a kiss on the cheek. He quickly did the same, then stepped backward. "I apologize for making you wait. It's been a busy twenty-four hours."

"Well, it could get even more busy, Keith." Diana waved to the left, indicating the nearby rockers. "Sit."

Keith did as he'd been bidden, taking the seat closest to her. Trudy settled to his left, also waiting.

With a put-upon sigh, Diana leaned forward and flipped over a number of pictures on the coffee table. "This was brought to my attention this morning." She pinned a narrow-eyed stare on Keith, her brown eyes holding a coolness that concerned him. "If the average person saw these, they could jump to the wrong conclusion."

Leaning forward, Keith picked up the pictures. As he flipped through them, he couldn't help but smile. They were all of him and Oliver at a restaurant. Judging by their clothes, it had been the past Saturday after their racquetball match and ensuing fun.

"Why are you smiling?" his mother snapped. "This is *bad*."

"This is actually good." Keith flipped to the picture he liked the most. While he sat staring at Oliver, open admiration on his face, his lover had a hand in the air and a huge smile on his face as he told a story about . . . something. "This is my lover, Oliver. I think I'll keep this one." Keith placed the others on the coffee table, doing his best to control his runaway heartbeat. "I was going to tell you about Oliver after discussing whatever trouble you were worried about. It seems I'm killing two birds with one stone." Ignoring his mother's pinched lips, Keith continued to smile and stated, "I need to add a plus-one to my reservation this weekend."

As much as Keith loved the squeal of delight Trudy issued, he worried about his mother's glacial stare. He wondered what was going on when she picked up her phone and sent a text.

Surely she remembers I'm bisexual . . . right?

CHAPTER TWELVE

"So, Keith watches *Survivor* with you." Jimmy smirked at Oliver. "Can you say match made in heaven?"

Scoffing, Oliver rolled his eyes as he turned on episode two of the second season. He still hardly believed that the man had started buying and watching seasons with him, even to help him through his damn near paralysis. Oliver couldn't think of any guy he'd dated in the past — when he had dated — that would have done that.

He's definitely one of the good ones.

"He'd never actually seen it before," Oliver finally admitted. Clearing his throat, he had to admit, "When he found me last night, I could barely put one foot in front of the other . . . *with* help." He sighed as he met Jimmy's worried gaze. "I'd never felt so helpless. If Clayton hadn't noticed. If you hadn't called Keith. If he hadn't dropped everything. God."

There were so many ifs in there.

"But Clayton did. I did. And Keith did." Jimmy took Oliver's hand. "And now, the cops are after the guy." His tone hardened as his eyes narrowed. "And that asshole is going to get what's coming to him."

Not wanting to discuss it further, Oliver nodded and said, "You're absolutely right." He did his best to add as much conviction in there as possible. Forcing a smile, he grabbed the bone broth drink Jimmy had made for him. "So, have you ever seen season two? Wasn't it before we discovered the show?"

Jimmy crossed his legs under him on the cushion and settled in. "Yep. I don't recognize any of these people." Cocking his head, he added, "Have they ever filmed in Australia after this season?"

While Oliver loved to consider himself a super fan, he had to shrug, admitting his ignorance. "I'd have to look it up."

Staring at him with wide eyes, Jimmy's feigned ignorance was totally over the top. "What?" He rested his hand over his chest. "You?"

"Oh, my god! Would you look at that guy? He's stealing food!" Oliver pointed at the screen, too engrossed in what was going on to give Jimmy shit. "That bastard."

"Oooohhh, he's gonna be in trub-bull." Jimmy sing-songed the last word, shaking his head. "He so better be the first one they vote off if they lose."

"I really don't remember much of this even though I watched it last night," Oliver mused as the episode continued. "How weird is that, right?"

Jimmy shrugged. "Well, your brain was a bit scrambled, so that's understandable." Then he knocked shoulders with Oliver. "Plus, you were in the arms of a hunky guy you're totally into." Giving him a quick wink before returning his attention to the TV, Jimmy added, "That'll totally mess up your focus of the show." He snickered.

Oliver gaped as he snapped his attention to Jimmy. "Oh my god! Have you been *Survivor* cheating on me?"

Immediately, Jimmy's cheeks began to pinken, and he wouldn't meet Oliver's gaze.

"Oh, you so have," Oliver pressed, a growl in his voice. "I can't believe it." He crossed his arms over his chest and grumbled, "You've been watching *Survivor* with Vance, then pretending you didn't and watching it again with me."

Jimmy suddenly burst out laughing. "Oh god," he gasped, resting his hand over his chest as he rocked and laughed.

"*Survivor* cheating? Yes." He grinned at Oliver. "I totally did, but only once." With tears streaming down his cheeks, his bestie told him, "We didn't even make it halfway through the episode before we were making out, then fucking, and when we came up for air, the show was over."

Joining Jimmy in his laughter, Oliver shook his head. "TMI, man," he teased, wiping away a stray tear. "TMI!"

Snorting, Jimmy tried to pull himself together. "Sorry, but we never lie to each other."

It was Oliver's turn to knock his shoulder into Jimmy's. "Yeah, yeah." Returning his attention to the TV, he murmured happily, "You're such a goof."

Jimmy just hummed, evidently not minding that label at all.

They fell silent, both smiling, as they both continued watching. Every once in a while, one of them would yell at a contestant, boo a choice, or cheer a decision. They discussed the merits of different characters and their actions.

By the time the credits rolled, they'd both agree they needed to make popcorn and order a pizza.

"Hey, do you think Keith has any beer around?" Jimmy called from the kitchen where he was rummaging in the pantry for popcorn. "Or wine?"

Laughing, Oliver was busy searching Keith's office for a piece of mail that would tell him the man's address. "I don't think he's going to like it if I have any alcohol," he admitted. "I had to puppy-dog eye him for a cup of coffee this morning."

Damn. Was it really less than five hours ago? Crazy!

"Awww, that's so sweet," Jimmy called back. "Okay. No alcohol. Ha! Found the popcorn."

"Didn't he text you his address?" Oliver hollered, having trouble finding what he wanted. The man was definitely very neat and organized.

"Yeah, but it's in my car's GPS." Jimmy appeared in the

doorway. "Want me to go out and look it up?"

Oliver shook his head. "No. It's gotta be around here some—"

The ring of the doorbell cut off anything he'd planned to say. A fissure of unease slithered up Oliver's spine. He desperately wished Keith was there as his heartrate spiked.

Jimmy frowned. "Are you expecting Ryan or Carl back?"

Shaking his head, Oliver rubbed his palms up and down his opposite arms. "Well, um, I guess I better check," he mused.

"No." Jimmy pointed at him. "I'll get it. You go find your phone."

"I can't leave you alone," Oliver countered.

"If it's that blond guy, I won't answer the door." Jimmy smiled encouragingly. "It has a peephole. Remember?"

While still feeling worried, Oliver nodded. "Right." He tried to remember that, before being attacked, he would never have been worried about answering a door. "But I'm just going to get my phone. Then I'll be right back up here."

Jimmy nodded as the doorbell chimed a third time. "Right."

Oliver moved as swiftly as he could through the house. Unfortunately, that wasn't very fast, considering he was still recovering. By the time he reached the kitchen where his phone was on the charger, sweat beaded on his brow and he was already panting.

Resting his hand on the table, Oliver tried to catch his breath. "Damn it," he grumbled. "This sucks."

After a few deep breaths, Oliver grabbed his phone and started toward the living room. He froze in the doorway when he saw the woman standing in the middle of the room talking to Jimmy. She wore a smart-looking skirt-suit, and her dark-brown hair had been weaved into an elegant French twist. The heels she sported only put her an inch or so shorter than Jimmy's five-foot-eleven, but she still seemed to be doing her best to stare imperiously down upon him.

Evidently, she caught Oliver's movement out of her eye. She turned and pinned him with a narrow-eyed stare of disdain. "You must be Oliver Kostroma."

"Yes." Oliver couldn't help the wariness in his tone.

Sniffing in obvious contempt, the woman pulled out a file. "This isn't the first time you've tried to wheedle your way into becoming a rich patron's kept man." She tossed the file onto the table. "If you're smart, you'll walk away, and it'll be your last attempt."

Pictures fell from the folder and slid across the table. While Oliver couldn't see them, he couldn't help but notice Jimmy's reaction. His eyes widened, and he lifted one hand to cover his mouth.

Smirking, the woman stated, "Do the right thing, Oliver. Walk away." The smile on her painted red lips appeared cruel. "Before more strident options need to be put into place."

Just that fast, the dark-haired woman pivoted on her heels and disappeared into the foyer. The slam of a door told Oliver that she'd left.

Confused about why Jimmy's face had gone so pale, Oliver started toward him . . . and whatever was in the pictures.

"There has to be another explanation," Jimmy claimed, snapping out of whatever stupor had held him. "No way is this what it looks like."

Oliver didn't want to look. Still, he had to. He turned his attention to the pictures strewn across the coffee table . . . and his heart nearly stopped.

Beads of sweat popped out on his forehead as he took in the contents. He felt as if his life was on replay. There, in full-color display, was Keith swinging a blonde woman around in his arms. One picture showed his wide smile and how his eyes were filled with joy. Another picture captured him kissing her cheek. The woman's cheeks were flushed, her expression one of pure happiness at seeing Keith.

"Oh my god," Oliver whispered, and he began struggling to breathe. "H-How could he . . . after what I told him?"

"Y-You told him about Rodger?" Jimmy stared at him in disbelief.

Oliver nodded. "I thought—"

He paused, casting his gaze around the living room, trying to make sense of his life. Could he truly have such bad karma? Or maybe he'd been an extremely horrible person in a past life?

Hell if he knew. He just—

Oliver's attention fell on a shelf full of pictures, some obviously of a winery. That wasn't what drew his attention, however. Instead, some of the others caught his eye.

"I'm so sorry, Oliver," Jimmy murmured, his tone forlorn. "I truly thought Keith was one of the good ones. Patrick would have definitely told us if he knew he was involved. He fooled us all. He—"

"Shhhh," Oliver snapped, holding up his hand. He kept his gaze locked on the shelf of pictures. "Look at this."

"What?"

Oliver stopped before the shelf. "This."

There were a few pictures that were clearly family portraits. The first three had a man and woman as well as a son and daughter. The family resemblance was pretty clear.

"Keith has never talked about his family." Oliver had shut down any talk of family in the past.

Touching the first that didn't include the father, Oliver knew he was looking at a young Keith—maybe in his early twenties. The girl was at least seven or eight years younger than him. Except, the woman in the last picture in the row matched the woman in the photos.

"This is his sister," Oliver whispered, glancing from the coffee table and back again. "But why would they pretend — " Just as fast, the answer clicked into place. "I'm black. I'm a man. I'm blue-collar." Scoffing, Oliver shook his head. "Take your pick."

"What are you saying?" Jimmy whispered from where he stood beside him. He glanced from Oliver to the pictures and back again, clearly confused. "What's going on?"

Oliver smiled sadly at Jimmy. "I'm being warned away from Keith." He waved at the pictures, taking in the hard lines around the mother's lips. Her smile was as fake as the day was long. Recalling the few words he'd overheard of Keith and his mother's conversation — a situation had come up — Oliver realized that *he* was the *situation*. "I'm guessing it's the mother. She doesn't want me to be with Keith. Take your guess as to why."

Scoffing derisively, Jimmy snarled out, "Well, she can kiss your black ass. You're just as good, hell, better than most people." Crossing his arms over his chest, he added, "Hell, probably better than *her*." Jimmy glared at Keith's mother in the picture. "Bet she's a right bitch."

Nodding slowly, Oliver had to agree with his friend. Still, these were his lover's family. He couldn't come between them. That wasn't a choice he should make for Keith.

Oliver took in a deep breath, then let it out slowly. He turned and smiled at Jimmy. "Will you take me home, please?"

"What?" Jimmy squeaked. "Why?" He waved his hand toward the pictures. "Because of this? You know it's bullshit."

"It *is* bullshit," Oliver agreed. "I know that, and you know that. Keith will know that." Shrugging, he had to add, "But the threat to Keith isn't bogus. She'll do something to hurt him if I'm in the picture, and I can't make the choice to stay without his say so. I need to think." As much as Oliver didn't want to leave Keith, he continued, "He'll call, and I'll talk to him about this then." When Jimmy opened his mouth, most likely to once again counter him, Oliver lifted his hands in placation. "He'll come home, see these pictures, and call me. I have no doubt." *God, please call me.* "But in the meantime, I also think that bitch who delivered these pictures is watching. We need to make her believe that the plan worked."

"Okay." Jimmy frowned at him. "I don't like it, but I understand it."

"Thank you." After a second of just standing there, Oliver stated, "I'm going to get my things."

Jimmy nodded once more, then moved with him.

Oliver gathered his cell phone charger, a couple of clothes items on the first floor, and that was it. He had no desire to drag his recovering body upstairs for a few changes of clothing. They could be replaced, or Keith would choose him and he would get them back.

Either way, it was just stuff.

As Oliver walked out of the house, locking the door behind him, he could feel his heart breaking a little. He didn't know when it had happened, but he'd made the mistake of falling for the man. With a sigh, Oliver didn't have to fake the tear that trickled down his cheek.

Oliver climbed into the passenger side and settled in the seat. Closing his eyes, he relaxed in the seat.

"Will you come to my place?" Jimmy asked softly as he started driving.

As tempting as that was, Oliver shook his head. "No. I don't want to impose." Flashing a smile Jimmy's way, he reminded, "You're newly engaged, remember?"

"Vance wouldn't care," Jimmy countered.

Even knowing that, Oliver still requested, "Please take me home."

They'd just turned out of the neighborhood onto the road

leading across town when their car lurched sideways. They both screamed as the car slammed into the ditch.

Oliver's body jerked sideways. His head slammed into the window. Pain slashed through him, and darkness took him.

Chapter Thirteen

"Get rid of him, or lose everything."

Keith gripped the wheel of his *BMW* and growled under his breath. How dare his mother threaten him, threaten what he was building with Oliver. Hell, she was even threatening Trudy, because if his sister didn't fall in line and cut Keith out of her life as Mother intended to do if Keith didn't obey, she would no longer inherit the vineyard—her life's work.

"Mother won't live forever." Keith winced upon mumbling the uncharitable words. "Damn it."

Shaking his head, Keith tried to figure out a way out of this mess . . . without giving up his lover. He knew that would be like cutting out his heart. For the first time in years, Keith felt alive. He had something to live for other than his work.

He loved it, having forgotten what that felt like.

His phone rang, echoing through his car's speakers. He almost ignored it, but on the off chance it could be Oliver, he checked who was incoming. Seeing Trudy's name on his screen, he sighed.

May as well get this over with.

"Hi, sis," Keith greeted softly. "Look. I totally understand. The vineyard is your priority."

"The vineyard is *a* priority, but not *the* priority," Trudy countered, sounding angry. Then her growl came through the line before she declared, "Besides, that bigoted old hag can't take the vineyard away from me."

Keith couldn't help but snicker. "Good word usage." He

quickly sobered, saying, "We both know that if you don't cut me out of the family just as she will if I don't walk away from Oliver, then she'll cut you out of her will, too, and you'll lose the vineyard."

Trudy heaved a sigh, sadness bleeding through. "Mother has always had her strange ideas, but I never thought it would come to this."

"I understand," Keith repeated. "I truly do. If you're not heading up the winery, it'll go downhill so fast. Mother doesn't understand the business."

A hard note crept into Trudy's voice as she stated, "Which is why I assure you that Mother can't take the vineyard away from me. Do you remember when I bought your percentage from you so you could open the law firm with Richard?"

"Yeah," Keith replied slowly. "That was . . . almost twelve years ago. What about it?"

"Well, Dad willed you thirty-four percent when he died. Where do you think he willed the other sixty-six percent?"

Confused, Keith answered, "Mother."

"Nope," Trudy responded glibly. "Even back then, Dad understood that Mom had no head for vines, so he only willed her thirty-three percent. *I* got the other thirty-three." After ushering a self-satisfied hum, Trudy claimed, "Thirty-three plus thirty-four is sixty-seven. I'm the majority owner. Mother can *not* take the vineyard from me. No matter what she does with her shares, the vineyard is mine."

"Damn," Keith whispered. "How come I didn't remember that?"

"Eh, you were pretty broken up at the time," Trudy reminded him gently. "Even though I followed him around the vineyard and you went to law school, you were still his only son."

Letting out a soft hum, Keith knew she was right. "Wow. Okay." Then he smiled faintly. "So, where do we go from here? Oh, hang on." Keith slowed down and carefully steered around the cones set up by the emergency services and police vehicles. A fissure of unease slid up his spine as he saw the crumpled rear fender and one working taillight sticking out of the ditch. "Damn. That looks like it hurt."

"What's going on?"

"My guess, a rear-end collision that sent someone into a deep irrigation ditch." Keith peered around the scene and frowned. "Hope they already took the second vehicle away and it wasn't a hit and run. That would suck."

"Bummer."

Keith silently agreed.

"Okay, so here's the deal, bestest lawyer bro," Trudy continued confidently. "Don't you worry about me or the vineyard. We're fine, and I will never turn my back on you. No matter what." After a second, Trudy stated, "The only thing you really need to be concerned about is your firm. If you're willing to deal with the fallout of having a male lover, partner, husband, whatever you end up being, then you follow your heart." Her voice took a slightly colder note as she stated, "But if you can't hack that, then you need to let that handsome chocolate thunder go before either of you get in any deeper."

Growling, Keith snapped, "Stop checking out my man. Oliver is mine." With a scoff, he added, "And even if it would affect my business, which it won't, I can earn more business. Oliver is worth it."

"Awww, my big bro is in love!" Trudy cried, sounding ridiculously happy. "That's wonderful."

"Yes, I am," Keith admitted. "But let's keep that between ourselves until I can tell—" Seeing his empty driveway, he felt his gut clench. "What the hell?"

"What's going on?"

"Um, Jimmy's gone," Keith answered, trepidation running

116

through him. "He was supposed to be staying with Oliver until I got home. There's someone after Oliver."

"You mean someone other than Mother?"

Gasping, Keith felt as if his heart skipped a beat. "Her text," he hissed. "What did she do?"

Without waiting for Trudy's response, Keith disconnected the call, saying, "I'll call you right back." He grabbed his phone and rushed from his *BMW*. He jogged up the steps and tried the door, oddly relieved to find it locked. After unlocking it, Keith rushed inside.

Keith ran into the living room but saw that the space was empty. Even the throw blanket had been folded and returned to its place. Except, then the coffee table caught his attention.

It *wasn't* empty.

Pictures were strewn across it. At first glance, they appeared innocuous enough. They were just pictures of him and his sister. He was twirling her around, happy to see her.

"Hell, that just happened today," Keith muttered. "What the fuck?"

Then Keith recalled Oliver's recounting of his past. A guy named Rodger had been involved with a woman for months before taking up with Oliver. Rodger had been using Oliver while courting a prospective fiancée.

"If I ever learn Rodger's last name," Keith snarled. While most of his work involved custody battles, they could get pretty nasty. He would be happy to use his expertise to rain hell down on the asshole who'd hurt Oliver . . . and who'd instilled such distrust in him.

Because Keith knew *that* was exactly what had to have been running through Oliver's mind to make him leave. The pictures made it appear that he was involved with Trudy. They were carefully clicked and manipulated to perfection.

Still, Keith couldn't help but search his home before going off half-cocked. He figured it was possible that they'd gone for a pizza run or something. The *Survivor* season two was still up on his TV screen, after all. Keith called Oliver's number as he made the rounds of the house.

The ice cream was still in the freezer, and Oliver's bag of clothes was still in the study.

That has to mean something. Right?

Then why the hell was Oliver's phone going straight to voicemail?

Keith double-checked, but he couldn't find the charger anywhere. Oliver must have taken it with him. If he had his phone off, that didn't bode well for things between them.

Just as Keith prepared to call Oliver's phone again—because he didn't have a better idea—his phone rang instead. His hope that it was Oliver crashed and burned. Instead, he saw that Ryan was calling him.

"Oliver isn't with me at the moment," Keith answered by way of greeting. "I'll need to call you—"

"Do you know where Oliver is?" Ryan cut in, his tone dark.

Grimacing, Keith had to admit, "Afraid not. I just got home. He was supposed to be here with Jimmy, but Jimmy's car is gone and so are they. I was about to call Jimmy." It wasn't totally the truth, but the idea had just popped into his head.

"Jimmy is in the hospital," Ryan told him. "His car was forced off the road just outside your neighborhood."

"What?" Keith felt as if his heart skipped a beat as he recalled the car in the ditch. "And Oliver?"

"According to eyewitnesses, Jimmy's car was forced off the road by a vehicle matching Dale's description," Ryan stated succinctly. "Oliver wasn't in the vehicle, but his charger was." After a second, Ryan finished, "We're not certain where he is."

Stumbling backward, Keith fell onto the sofa behind him. "Dale has him?" he whispered, anguish filling his tone. "But . . . but . . . you had guys out looking for him."

"Yeah, we did, but no one has seen him," Ryan admitted. His voice sounded gruff, strange, as if he were barely holding it together himself. "I don't know what happened, but if I can figure out if someone slacked, I'll—"

Keith's phone chimed, pulling his attention away from Ryan. "That's Oliver's ringtone," he whispered before pulling his phone from his ear. He quickly pulled up the text.

Taken by Dale. So sorry. Old apartment building on Lexington and

"And?" Keith whispered. "And what?"

"What'd it say?" Ryan demanded, shouting to get his attention. "What's going on?"

Keith quickly relayed Oliver's message. "But I just called him, and it went straight to voicemail," he muttered, thinking quickly. Something didn't make sense. "Wait." It hit him, and he started back outside to his car. "Oliver's phone died last night. Jimmy brought Oliver's phone charger as well as clothes and food. He must have just turned it back on." An idea clicked in Keith's mind, and he ordered, "Ping Oliver's phone."

"Already on it," Ryan declared. "We'll have a location shortly." Evidently, the detective heard Keith firing up his vehicle, for he demanded, "Where the fuck do you think you're going?"

"I'm going to drive Lexington looking for old apartment buildings," Keith replied, thinking the answer would have been obvious.

"Don't tip our hand, Keith," Ryan snapped at him. "Besides, what the hell do you think you'll accomplish? You have no law enforcement or military training. What if he has a gun?"

Keith growled under his breath. He didn't want to think reasonably. He wanted to figure out where on Lexington that asshole Dale could have taken his man.

"Where was that?" Ryan didn't seem to be talking to him.

"Lexington and Pine? Got it. Okay everything. Hostage situation. We—Oh, fuck. You're still listening, aren't you, Keith?"

"Of course I'm fucking listening, Ryan." Keith grinned. "Meet you at Lexington and Pine."

Before the cussing detective could yell at him further, Keith closed the connection. He ignored Ryan's attempt to call him back in favor of contacting Vance. The man picked up after the first ring.

"Have they found Oliver?"

As much as it warmed Keith that Vance's initial instinct was to ask about Oliver, he didn't have good news . . . not yet. "They've pinged his phone's location," Keith told Vance. "I'm headed in that direction and hope they'll have him secured before I arrive." After a heartbeat, he added, "I'm so sorry this happened, Vance. How's Jimmy?" Keith hadn't yet heard.

Vance sighed deeply. "He'll be okay. A concussion and a badly sprained right wrist, most likely from trying to brace himself as they crashed."

"I'm glad to hear that," Keith replied honestly. He knew Oliver would want to know as soon as they spoke. *If he'll speak to me.* That brought him back to the other reason for his call—a very selfish reason. "Look, I know I'm being an ass for asking this, but when Jimmy wakes, will you tell him that those pictures he and Oliver saw weren't what they seemed?" Keith hurried to add, "The blonde in the pictures is my sister, Trudy. I hadn't seen her for a couple of weeks, and we—"

"Jimmy knows," Vance cut in, his voice catching Keith's attention. "They both knew. Oliver figured it out."

Pain stabbed through Keith's chest for a new reason, and he had to stop his car on the side of the road to keep from losing control. "Then *why*?" he whispered. "Why would Oliver leave if he knew?"

Vance chuckled softly. "For the same reason it took Jimmy so long to agree to move in with me way back in the day," he explained. "He didn't want to come between family." After a few seconds, Vance added, "That has to be your choice. To accept Oliver despite family objections."

"Now that Oliver has given me half a chance, he *is* my family," Keith declared, frowning at nothing. "And as soon as I get him in my arms again, I'm gonna figure out a way to convince him of that."

"Good," Vance replied. "I'll tell Jimmy. He'll feel better for it." Then he growled and added, "Now go find that asshole and kick his ass for me."

Scoffing softly, Keith eased his *BMW* back onto the road. "I wish it could be me to—Holy fuck!" Stopping at a red light, he stared at the car to his right in the left-hand turn lane. He practically gaped. A quick glance at the license plate confirmed it. "That's Dale's car."

Acting on instinct, when the light gave Dale's car a green arrow, Keith checked out the driver. *Definitely Dale.* He didn't see anyone else, but that didn't stop him.

As soon as Dale was halfway through the intersection, Keith gunned his engine. He angled his driver's side headlight to slam into the other vehicle's driver's side fender. Their cars jolted, throwing Keith against his seatbelt. He heard the scrape of metal and saw the way his front end slid to the edge of the driver's side door.

Lifting his hands, Keith barely avoided the headache that the deploying airbag would have caused. He shook his head, trying to clear his swimming senses. With trembling fingers, he reached for his seatbelt clasp. He found it, released his belt, then tried his door. That took another three tries before he remembered to hit the unlock button first.

Keith stumbled out of his car. At the last second, he reached down and snagged a tire iron that he'd placed between his driver's seat and the door as soon as he'd bought the vehicle. It wasn't to his *BMW*, and it hadn't moved in three years, but his father's advice on self-defense had never left his mind.

Hefting his weapon, Keith stumbled more than stalked around the hood of Dale's car. He saw how his vehicle's front fender had smashed in the corner of the driver's side door, so he knew the asshole wouldn't be able to get out that way. Peering through the passenger side window, Keith took in Dale's bloody head where it rested against the wheel.

"Hey, buddy," someone yelled. "Are you okay?"

Not trusting that Dale was actually unconscious, Keith didn't remove his attention away from him as he hollered back, "Yeah, I'm okay. Call the police. This man is a fugitive."

That was when the quietest of thumps caught his attention.

Ignoring Dale, Keith stumbled to the back of the vehicle. "Oliver?" he yelled, staring at the trunk. "You in there, babe?"

"Keith?"

Keith grinned, fighting back a laugh upon hearing Oliver's clearly disbelieving tone. "Yep. It's me, babe. Is this gonna be an ongoing thing?" he teased as he swept an eye over the area. "Cause if it is, I might have to take some more self-defense classes."

Then, to Keith's ever-loving shock, Oliver called, "I love you."

Allowing his eyelids to slide closed for an instant, Keith answered, "I love you, too, Oliver."

Any other talk was drowned out by the sound of sirens.

Ryan and Carl arrived, and things happened pretty fast after that.

EPILOGUE

"Oh god, what are you going to do?"

Oliver stared wide-eyed up at his lover. He saw the hunger in Keith's dark eyes, which caused his gut to tighten. A shiver of anticipation worked down his spine as his cock jerked and twitched.

"I think it's time to move this relationship along," Keith rumbled, crawling toward him on the bed. "Don't you?"

Sweeping his gaze over Keith's sexy, naked frame, Oliver licked his lips. "Y-Yes." His gut clenched as much as his chute. Keith was a big man, and it had been so damn long.

"Good."

Then, to Oliver's surprise, Keith reached over to the nightstand and pulled out not a condom and lube, but a piece of paper. He eased onto the comforter next to Oliver and held it out to him.

Confused, Oliver took it. A quick sweep told him what he was reading. He stared in shock. When the bed jostled, he jerked his attention back to Keith.

Oliver's jaw sagged when he saw the keyring dangling from his naked lover's forefinger. "Oh my god," Oliver whispered. "A-Are you r-really asking me to move in with you?"

Keith nodded, his smile exuding confidence. "I am." Easing up the bed, he reached over and set the keyring on the nightstand that—for the last month—Oliver had been thinking of as *his* nightstand. "You sleep here five out of seven nights a week," Keith pointed out. "I want to make that permanent." While he cradled Oliver's jaw in his large hand, his expression sobered. "I miss you when you're not here, and I don't like it. Please, move in with me. You can show me your test or don't. Tell me you're clean, and I'm going to fuck you raw. It's well past time."

Sucking in a sharp gasp, Oliver felt arousal surge through his mind. He struggled to process everything Keith was saying. His focus danced from Keith's lips to his eyes to his body and back again.

"Wow," Oliver whispered, knowing he needed to say something. "I-I-I . . ." He blew out a sharp breath. "I'm clean, but are you sure?"

"Sure about going without condoms?" Keith asked bluntly.

Oliver nodded. "We've never even fucked yet."

As much as they'd done together over the past few weeks as Oliver had healed and everything had been sorted with Dale as well as Keith's mother, they hadn't fucked. Yes, there had been plenty of penetration with fingers and tongues, but their dicks hadn't been part of that. Instead, they'd stuck to hand jobs, blowjobs, rub-offs, and everything in between.

In truth, Oliver was beginning to think fucking just wasn't Keith's thing.

God, does this mean I'm wrong? Please, let it mean I'm wrong.

When Keith teased his fingertip over Oliver's scalp between braids, tingles shot down his neck, drawing a gasp from Oliver. A smug smile curved Keith's lips as he swept his gaze over him.

"Well," Keith drawled. "You had a week of healing, so of course I had to be gentle." Pinning Oliver with a look that was more anger than heat, he continued, "Then that fiasco with my mother." He growled as he shook his head. "Trying to make you think I was involved with my sister. Disgusting."

Oliver winced sympathetically.

Keith's mother had sent more pictures when the first ones hadn't worked. They'd been older, from when they'd been hanging out in the vineyard together. It was as if the woman was trying to prove a deep meaningful relationship that Oliver had been intruding upon.

Considering Oliver had seen through it right off, it hadn't come close to working, but boy, had Keith been pissed. He'd warned his mother to cease with her meddling. When that hadn't done the trick, Keith had threatened to sue her with defamation of Oliver's character.

At that, Diana had backed off. Evidently, even her name anywhere near a court case, especially one that made her appear intolerant, did the trick. She still hadn't added a plus-one to Keith's reservation for her party, so Keith had refused to go.

Boy, had that been the talk of the social pages — Keith Ryzor snubs his mother's party.

Suddenly, Diana had become much more welcoming and tolerant.

Oliver didn't trust it, but he would play nice until proven otherwise.

"Now, it's time to give us what we both want," Keith continued. "I'm going to open you up, sliding my fingers deep into your ass over and over, before replacing them with my cock." Holding Oliver's gaze, his deep brown eyes burning with passion, Keith added, "And I want that to be bare because you've promised yourself to me for all time." After nipping Oliver's jaw, Keith asked huskily, "You in our bed each night, in our house each day, and my partner against the world. Does that work for you?"

Holding Keith close, Oliver declared, "Yes . . . to everything."

As Keith did everything he'd promised, causing Oliver to writhe on their sheets with ecstasy, he knew he'd never made a wiser decision.

About the Author

Charlie started writing fantasy when she was eight, and after stumbling onto her first erotic romance at age nineteen, she realized her true calling. She now focuses on writing gay erotic romance, normally of the paranormal variety, with heroes of all kinds. With the help and support of her husband, Charlie finally fulfilled one of her life-long goals . . . move to acreage with her horses. You can often find her curled up with her laptop and a cup of tea or glass of wine, creating her next adventure. Charlie enjoys exploring the mountains of her new Oregon home on horseback, 4-wheeler, or motorcycle.

She can be reached at ch.richards2010@yahoo.com

Or visit her at www.charlie-richards.com.

www.ingramcontent.com/pod-product-compliance
Lightning Source LLC
Chambersburg PA
CBHW060629130626
46555CB00002B/723